“Who are you? What ridiculous story you told my butler?”

How many different surrogates did they have, that Alex didn’t immediately know who she was? Frowning, she blinked in bewilderment. “I’m Rosalie. Rosalie B-Brown.”

“Well. Rosalie, Rosalie Brown,” he mocked, “is this some kind of joke? Are you truly claiming to be pregnant with my baby?”

Claiming? She frowned. “You know I am.”

“And how could that be?” he said scornfully, folding his powerful arms. “I never cheated on my wife, not in three years of our marriage, not once, not even when she—”

He cut himself off, his jaw clenching.

Rosalie gaped at him. “I saw your signature on the surrogacy contract!”

“Contract?” he growled. “What are you talking about?”

Was it possible—he didn’t know?

USA TODAY bestselling author **Jennie Lucas**'s parents owned a bookstore, so she grew up surrounded by books, dreaming about faraway lands. A fourth-generation Westerner, she went east at sixteen to boarding school on a scholarship, wandered the world, got married, then finally worked her way through college before happily returning to her hometown. A 2010 RITA® Award finalist and 2005 Golden Heart® Award winner, she lives in Idaho with her husband and children.

Books by Jennie Lucas

Harlequin Presents

Christmas Baby for the Greek
Her Boss's One-Night Baby

Conveniently Wed!

Chosen as the Sheikh's Royal Bride

One Night With Consequences

Claiming His Nine-Month Consequence

Secret Heirs of Billionaires

Carrying the Spaniard's Child

Secret Heirs and Scandalous Brides

The Secret the Italian Claims
The Heir the Prince Secures
The Baby the Billionaire Demands

Visit the Author Profile page
at Harlequin.com for more titles.

Jennie Lucas

CLAIMING THE VIRGIN'S BABY

HARLEQUIN® PRESENTS®

Recycling programs for this product may not exist in your area.

ISBN-13: 978-1-335-89364-2

Claiming the Virgin's Baby

This edition published by arrangement with Harlequin Books S.A.

For questions and comments about the quality of this book, please contact us at CustomerService@Harlequin.com.

Harlequin Enterprises ULC
22 Adelaide St. West, 40th Floor
Toronto, Ontario M5H 4E3, Canada
www.Harlequin.com

Printed in U.S.A.

CLAIMING THE VIRGIN'S BABY

To Julie Sonveau and all my fellow travelers to Mont-Saint-Michel. You know who you are ;)

CHAPTER ONE

PANIC. FEAR. BITTER REGRET.

Those were the things that Rosalie Brown felt as she looked down at her seven-months'-pregnant belly.

She took a deep breath. She'd thought she could do this—be a surrogate mother for a childless married couple. She'd convinced herself that at the end of her pregnancy she'd be able to joyfully give the baby into the arms of his true, loving family.

She'd been a fool.

Burning tears lifted to Rosalie's eyes. Wrapping her hands over the wrinkled cotton of her sundress, she cradled her baby bump, her heart in her throat.

For the last seven months, as this baby had grown inside her, she'd felt him kick and move. She'd gone to ultrasounds and gotten in the habit of talking to him out loud as she took long walks along the edge of San Francisco Bay, morning and evening, rain and shine. As the winter fog rolled in, as the spring sunshine sparkled on the water, she'd come to love this baby.

Secretly.

Stupidly.

Rosalie blinked fast. When she'd seen the fertility clinic's ad looking for surrogates, she'd been in a bad place, grief stricken, newly unemployed and unable to ever go home again. When she'd seen the ad, she'd thought it was a miracle: a way not just to help pay her rent for a few months, but to truly do something good in the world. The best way—the only way—to get past her own blinding guilt and pain.

So she'd met the prospective mother, a beautiful, chic Italian woman who'd had tears in her eyes as she spoke of her husband's desire for a child. "Please," the woman had whispered in huskily accented English, "you're the only one who can help us." For the first time in months, Rosalie had felt something other than despair. She'd signed the surrogacy contract that very day.

It was only a few weeks later, when she'd first started to surface from the fog of grief, that she'd had second thoughts. She'd realized she'd be giving up her own baby, not just carried by her body, but even related to her biologically. Yes, she would conceive the baby in a medical clinic, and she'd yet to meet the biological father, but would that make the child any less hers?

After just one artificial insemination attempt,

Rosalie had realized it was a horrible mistake. She'd known she couldn't be a surrogate after all. She'd decided to tell them to forget it.

But it was already too late.

She was pregnant. Pregnant on the first try. With a child that, by her own signed contract, she'd be forced to give away at birth.

For the last seven months, Rosalie had tried to convince herself the baby wasn't really hers. She'd told herself the baby belonged to Chiara Falconeri and her husband, Alex. This was *their* baby. Not hers.

But every part of Rosalie—heart and body and soul—violently disagreed. Until finally, she could bear it no longer. Last week, she'd gotten a passport for the first time in her life. She'd booked an international flight.

And she'd flown here today, to Venice, in an act that could only be described as pure lunacy. For how would Rosalie ever convince the Italian couple to tear up the contract and let her keep her baby?

"Signora?"

She looked up at the smiling young Italian man in the striped shirt, holding his hand to help her out of the vaporetto, which had shuttled them across the lagoon from the Marco Polo airport. A hot gust of wind hit her yellow sundress, already wrinkled from being crammed into a middle seat in the airplane's back row for a fourteen-hour flight. The small ferry rocked beneath her, or maybe she was just dizzy from stress and lack of sleep.

"Help with bag?" the young man asked politely.

"No," she said, clinging to her small overnight bag on her shoulder. *"Grazie."* It was the only word in Italian she knew, other than food words like spaghetti or gelato.

"Ciao, bella." She felt the young man's eyes follow her as she went up the gangplank, and she felt self-conscious of her hugely pregnant shape. She obviously wasn't actually beautiful. Italian men must call every woman *bella*, she decided, as a mark of warmth and respect. She liked the country already.

At least she *would*, if she could just convince the Italian couple to let her keep her baby. How hard could that be?

Yeah, right. Rosalie had a hollow feeling in her chest as she followed the crowd of tourists off the vaporetto and into the city, past charming outdoor cafés and shops selling brightly colored glass and Venetian masks. For a moment, she looked up at the city—Venice, city of dreams, La Serenissima.

She'd grown up on a small Northern California farm, until she'd moved to nearby San Francisco for a job. She'd never imagined she might someday travel to the other side of the world. She was dazzled by the fairy-tale Renaissance buildings, the romantic Juliet balconies, the canals sparkling like diamonds beneath the hot Italian sun.

Narrowing her eyes, she shook her head with a sigh. Who cared about exotic locales or fairy-tale dreams? She was here for one reason: to try to keep her baby.

She had to convince them. She *had* to. Fiercely, Rosalie focused on the map on her phone. She left the crowds pushing south to Saint Mark's Square, turning instead onto a quiet narrow street, then another. She followed the directions to the address from the contract, crossing a narrow bridge, far beyond the tourist hordes to the quiet Piazza di Falconeri.

With every step, she felt sweatier and more wrinkled. She'd only met Chiara Falconeri once at the clinic in California, and she'd never met the husband at all. But she knew there was no way that Alex Falconeri would call her *bella* as the other Italian man had. Not after Rosalie asked to take his son.

She stopped in front of a wrought-iron gate within a tall stone wall. Behind it, she could see a leafy green courtyard filled with plants and trees, and behind that, a discreet palazzo. This was it. For a second, her knees went weak beneath her. Then she thought of her desperation. Tugging her bag more firmly on her shoulder, she pressed the bell.

A cold voice came over the intercom. *"Sì?"*

Feeling awkward speaking to a stone wall, she said, "Um… I'd like to see—to speak to Mr. and Mrs. Falconeri, please."

"*Mr.* Falconeri?" The man's voice sounded scandalized, with an accent that reminded her of the English butler in *Downton Abbey.* "Do you have an appointment?"

"No, but they'll wish to see me." She hoped.

A sniff. "And who are you?"

"I'm—I'm Rosalie Brown. I'm their surrogate. I'm having their baby."

Dead silence on the other end of the intercom.

"Hello?" she ventured finally. "Is anyone there?" Still no answer. "Please, I've come all the way from California. If you could just ask Mrs. Falconeri, she can explain—"

There was a buzzing sound, and the gate suddenly snapped open. With a gulp, she pushed inside.

The courtyard was shadowy, quiet and green, and seemed a world away from the rest of crowded, treeless Venice. She heard birdsong as she went through the small garden to an elaborate door. But even as she reached up to knock, the door opened in front of her hand. A supercilious white-haired man, who was bent over and looked as if he had to be at least a hundred and fifty years old, looked up at her.

"You may come in." She recognized the quivery British voice. Beneath bushy white eyebrows, his gaze fell to her pregnant belly with a frown.

"Um… Thanks." Nervously, Rosalie entered the foyer and felt the welcome relief of air-conditioning cooling her overheated skin. She bit her lip, then said hesitantly, "Are you Mr. Falconeri?"

"I?" The elderly man coughed. "I am Collins, the butler. The *conte* is my employer."

"Conte?" she repeated, confused.

"Alexander Falconeri is the Conte di Rialto," he replied pointedly. "Strange you do not know who he is, if you are having his baby." His voice indicated how doubtful he was of that claim.

"Oh." Great. So her baby's father was apparently royalty of some kind. Like she needed to feel more insecure than she already did. Tilting back her head, Rosalie looked up at painted frescos of angels above the antique crystal chandelier soaring high overhead.

"This way, Miss Brown." The butler led her past a sweeping staircase and down a wide hallway, then through double doors, ten feet high, into a gilded salon. She gaped, looking around her at the Louis XIV furniture, an oil portrait over the marble fireplace and large windows overlooking a canal. "Wait here, if you please."

After he left, Rosalie paced nervously in the salon, uncertain where to stand or sit or look. A palace like this was totally foreign to her experience, nothing like the tiny apartment in San Francisco she'd shared with three other girls, or before that, her family's farm in Northern California, with its hundred-year-old farmhouse, crammed to the gills with mismatched furniture.

All very flammable, as it turned out…

She felt queasiness rise inside her and pushed the thought away. She forced herself to focus only on the room around her. This furniture, too, looked as if it had been handed down through generations, but very differently than how her loving, lived-in family home had been. Every chair in here, every table, looked priceless, almost untouchable—she eyeballed a gilded antique settee—and very uncomfortable.

With a sigh, she looked up at the portrait above the marble fireplace. The man in the painting, no doubt some long-ago Falconeri ancestor, looked down at her even more scornfully than the butler had. *You don't belong here*, the bewigged man's sneer seemed to say to her. And shivering, she agreed with him. No. She didn't. And neither did her baby.

There was no way she could allow her child to be raised in a museum like this. Rosalie gripped the leather strap of her bag. She'd recently discovered that surrogacy was illegal in Italy. A fact which Chiara and Alex Falconeri had obviously known when they'd decided to hire a surrogacy clinic in more lenient California.

But the thought of trying to use that to her advantage made her knees shake. No. She couldn't. Could she? Absolutely not. She'd never threatened anyone in her life.

But to keep her baby—?

"Who are you and what do you want?"

Hearing the low growl behind her, Rosalie whirled to face the man who'd just entered the salon door.

He was tall, powerfully built, with broad shoulders and a muscular shape. His hair was dark and mussed. His eyes were black and they burned right through her. Rosalie gripped the edge of the marble fireplace mantel for support as her knees trembled beneath her.

"You are—Alex Falconeri?" she croaked.

His dark eyes narrowed as he stalked into the room, then stopped directly in front of her. He was dressed all in black, a button-down shirt, perfectly tailored trousers, and leather shoes with a dull shine. His stark clothing seemed perfect for a palace like this—and totally wrong for real life, for the hot, sunny Italian weather outside, on the last day in May.

"You didn't answer my question." The man's gaze was a weapon, freezing her in place as he slowly looked her over. "Who are you? What is this ridiculous story you told my butler?"

How many different surrogates did they have that he didn't immediately know who she was?

Frowning, she blinked in bewilderment. "I'm Rosalie. Rosalie B-Brown."

"Well. Rosalie, Rosalie Brown," he mocked, "Is this some kind of joke? Are you truly claiming to be pregnant with my baby?"

Claiming? She frowned, bewildered. "You know I am."

"And how could that be?" he said scornfully, folding his powerful arms. "I never cheated on my wife, not in three years of marriage, not once, not even when she—"

He cut himself off, his jaw clenching.

Rosalie gaped at him. "I saw your signature on the surrogacy contract!"

"Contract?" he growled. "What are you talking about?"

Was it possible—he didn't know?

"Your wife—Mrs. Falconeri—I mean, the countess or whatever she's called, hired me through the surrogacy clinic in San Francisco last November. She told me you were—" she hesitated "—um, too busy to leave Italy. But she said you were happily married, and all you needed was a child to make your happiness complete."

"Happy?" He looked at her incredulously. "You cannot have actually met my wife. She would never have said that."

"Well—she said that once I had the baby, you'd be happy, because a baby was all you wanted.

And she said once I gave birth, she could finally be happy too."

Alex Falconeri stared at her coldly.

She licked her lips. "Just ask her," she said weakly. "She's the one who arranged everything. She—"

"I can't ask her anything," he bit out. His black eyes narrowed, hard as stone. "My wife is dead. In a car accident four weeks ago—"

"I'm so sorry—" Rosalie gasped.

"With her lover," he finished. "So I know everything you're saying is a lie."

Alexander Falconeri, the Conte di Rialto, stared at the beautiful young pregnant woman in the salon of his palazzo.

She was obviously lying. Her ridiculous story couldn't be true. Even Chiara wouldn't, couldn't, have done what this girl claimed. Create a child through a surrogate, without Alex's knowledge? No. Impossible.

Was it?

Impossible, he repeated to himself harshly. The girl claimed to have been impregnated in some fertility clinic in San Francisco. How could an American clinic even have gotten hold of Alex's DNA?

It had to be a trick.

Now *that*, he could believe. Chiara was—had been—clever and ruthless. For two years, she'd desperately wanted a divorce. Not just that, she'd wanted to take his fortune with her.

Alex had refused. He saw no reason to accept a divorce, much less tear up the prenup and meekly give her his inheritance. She'd done nothing to deserve it, and besides, he'd spoken vows. A man without honor was no man at all. For him, marriage, happy or unhappy, was forever.

Chiara had felt differently. After her wealthy father had died, a year into their marriage, she'd received her eagerly awaited inheritance and saw no reason to remain married to Alex. She'd been desperate to be free, so she could marry the penniless, drug-addicted musician she'd loved for years.

But she'd soon realized that even her large inheritance wouldn't last long, not the way she and Carraro bled money on their jet-set lifestyle. Her married lover had hinted that only a truly spectacular fortune could tempt him to leave his wife, and suddenly, a mere divorce wasn't enough for Chiara. She'd demanded that Alex forget their prenuptial agreement, and instead give her half his family's fortune.

When Alex had refused, she'd vengefully flaunted her affair, rubbing his nose in it, drunkenly partying with her lover in all the hot spots of Venice and Rome. She'd done everything possible to force Alex's hand.

But he'd refused to give in. Why should he?

Finally, in furious desperation, she'd threatened blackmail. Alex was scornful. He knew she had nothing to blackmail him with—he'd never betrayed her, never broken any law.

But a child.

She knew he wanted children. He was the last of his direct line. His family, powerful for five hundred years, had dwindled to only Alex and a distant cousin, Cesare. If he had no children, the title of Conte di Rialto would die with him.

But having an heir had seemed more and more unlikely, as he and Chiara had stopped sharing a bed long ago. For the last two years, he'd grimly waited for her to come to her senses and return to their marriage. He'd thought they could still have a partnership. He didn't need to love her. In fact, it was better if he did not.

But Chiara must have known that if she'd surprised him with a biological child, Alex would have been willing to surrender anything—his honor, his fortune—to protect his own flesh and blood.

Could she have actually done what this girl claimed?

"I'm so sorry about your wife," the American girl said now, interrupting his thoughts. Reaching out, she put her hand gently on his wrist. "Even if you had…problems in your marriage—" she stumbled over the words, then took a deep breath "—I'm sure you loved her very much."

She was sure of *what*? Shocked, Alex looked down at the small hand over his wrist.

It was a conventional gesture, meant to offer comfort. But comfort was the last thing he felt. The touch of her hand caused a sizzle to spread through his body, from his fingertips to his toes and everywhere in between.

Why would his body react that way to this girl—this stranger?

There was no special magic in it, Alex told himself harshly. It was an instinctive reaction, nothing more. It had been too long since he'd had sex. Years. His marriage had never been about passion, even from the beginning. Their union had been about merging old families, old vineyards. He'd barely known anything about Chiara, except that she was beautiful and from a distinguished family, and that she brought the nearby Vulpato Winery as a dowry. The few times they'd made love it had felt mechanical, perfunctory. And within months of their wedding day, even that had stopped entirely.

That was nearly three years ago.

Was there any wonder his body was reacting now to the slightest touch? The slightest care?

He yanked his hand away. She blushed in pretty confusion.

She was almost *too* pretty, with her expressive brown eyes and dark hair pulled up in a long ponytail. She wore a yellow sundress that hugged her lushly pregnant curves. Her legs were tanned and slender, all the way to her simple leather sandals. Her face was bare of makeup, and she wore no jewelry at all.

"But—I don't understand any of this." She looked at the large, worn-looking bag hanging on her shoulder. "The clinic wasn't notified of your wife's death, or at least I wasn't. And she said you were happy together—" The girl took an unsteady breath. "I'm sorry. You don't have to talk about it. I can only imagine your grief."

"No. You can't." She couldn't, because he wasn't feeling any. His whole body felt tight. "And I don't know anything about your clinic."

"You said she died in—in an accident?"

"Yes." *If you could call it accidental to get drunk and stoned with one's lover and drive on a curvy cliff road on a rainy night.* "Four weeks ago. You didn't hear? It was in the news."

He watched the girl as he spoke, waiting for some hint of recognition. For weeks, Chiara's death had been reported gleefully in the Italian and French media. It was the perfect bit of gossip for the start of summer, a juicy scandal to see the proud Conte di Rialto, the former playboy who before his marriage had been the despair of every actress and debutante in Europe, for the last two years brought low by his wife's endless public betrayals. Chiara's death had been the perfect end to the gossipy news story, dying with her lover in a spectacular fireball on the French Riviera.

But even before that, everyone on earth, it seemed—friends, acquaintances, total strangers—had asked Alex point-blank why he didn't just divorce her. He'd tried once or twice to explain about honor and the seriousness of vows, but even his friends didn't understand. *Promises are all well and good, Alex*, they'd said, shaking their heads, *but your wife is making a fool of you. Honor doesn't demand that you keep your wedding vows. Honor demands you divorce the cheating harlot!*

But this young woman's luminous dark eyes were full of anguished sympathy.

He hated her kindness.

It was an act. It had to be. There was no way she could be telling the truth about her baby's parentage, because there was no way a California clinic could have gotten his DNA without his knowledge or consent. Perhaps Chiara had found some struggling actress in LA who was already pregnant, and convinced her to play the role of a lifetime.

"I hope she paid you in advance," Alex said through gritted teeth. The girl blinked, her expression bewildered.

"What?"

"For whatever deal you made with my dear departed wife." He bared his teeth in a smile.

"She hired you, did she not? To come to Venice and pretend you were pregnant with my child?"

Gripping the strap of her bag, which was digging into her bare shoulder beside the thin strap of her sundress, she said in a wavering voice, "You don't believe me?"

The tremble of her voice, the unshed tears shining in her eyes. Oh, the girl was good. He'd give her that. Such an accomplished little actress, he expected he'd probably see her on television someday, accepting a gold statuette. "That you've conceived my baby in a test tube?"

"Artificial insemination," she mumbled, her cheeks turning pink.

"Miss—what was your name again?"

"Rosalie Brown."

"Miss Brown." Alex lifted an eyebrow. "I'll pay you double what Chiara did, if you'll admit you're lying."

"Lying?"

"Admit I'm not the father of your baby." He paused, tilting his head as he considered her. "That is, if you're even pregnant at all."

"Not pregnant?" Her voice was indignant. "Feel this!"

Grabbing his hand, she placed it on the swell of her belly. He half expected to discover soft padding, nothing more. Instead, he felt her belly's warmth and firmness. He pulled his hand back in surprise.

She glared at him. "Of course I'm pregnant. Why would I lie?"

"Girl or boy?" he challenged, a little shaken.

"What difference does it make? A boy. He'll be born in two months. You're the father."

"And you've come for a payout," he guessed grimly. His mind was whirling. "You were already pregnant when Chiara found you. But she promised you a good deal of money if you could come to Venice and make me believe I was the father, so she'd get her divorce."

"She wanted a divorce?"

"But when you heard she was dead, you were afraid you wouldn't get paid," he continued relentlessly. "So now you're hoping I'll pay you to go away."

"What? No! You've got it all wrong!"

Alex turned toward the grand piano, topped by dozens of framed pictures his parents had taken with celebrities and politicians long ago. It was strange to see his mother and father smiling together in pictures, when he had no memory of them doing that when they were alive. "Then what do you want, Miss Brown?"

Rosalie stared at him, her lovely face pale. He was tantalized once more by his attraction for her, the shape of her, her expressive eyes, deep pools of midnight scattered with faraway stars. She took a deep breath.

"I want *you* to go away," she whispered. "That's

why I came. That's why I just got a passport and traveled across the ocean for the first time in my life. I want this baby to be mine. Because he *is* mine. He's my son."

Alex's jaw fell. He recovered quickly. "You mean, you want my money—"

"No. All I want is my baby." Reaching into her worn leather bag, she pulled out a small roll of dollar bills wrapped by a rubber band. She held it out to him. "Here's what your wife gave me for pregnancy expenses. You can have it back. All of it."

Bewildered, he took the wad of bills. He looked down at the money. It seemed a very small amount. He lifted his head.

"You don't want anything from me?" he said slowly.

Rosalie Brown shook her head. A beam of sunlight burst through the salon's large window, glazing all the old furniture with gold, making the room briefly seem warm and alive.

"Go, then," Alex said hoarsely. "I don't know anything about your baby. There's no way I can be the father. So just get the hell out."

He expected her to respond with angry words.

Instead, Rosalie suddenly flung her arms around him in a tearfully grateful embrace. With a sob, she kissed him fiercely and lingeringly on the cheek.

"Thank you," she whispered, her lips brushing his ear. "Oh, thank you."

Alex felt the softness of her full breasts against his ribs, the push of her belly against his groin. He breathed in the scent of her dark hair, like vanilla and orange blossoms.

Electricity sizzled through his body, like a burst of heat and sunlight of summer after a long, cold, dead winter.

Rosalie drew back, looking up at him, and he felt the rush of cold air against his body where her warmth had just been. Tears streaked down her cheeks as she choked out, "You don't know what this means to me. I was afraid to even hope." Reaching into her bag, she pushed a document into his hands. "Please sign that and send it to the medical clinic in San Francisco. Just so they don't give me any trouble." Wiping her tears, she tried to smile. "Thank you. You're a good man," she whispered, and turning, she left.

Alex stared after her in shock. Then he looked down at the paper in his hands. It was a legal document that would sever all his parental rights, according to California law.

Why would Rosalie Brown come all the way to Venice, claim to be the mother of his child, but not ask him for any money?

He looked at the small roll of American dollars in his hand. In fact, she'd given money to *him*. None of this made sense.

Unless her story was true.

But it couldn't be. Because however much Chiara might have wished to put a diabolical plan like this in motion, how could she? There was no way he could be the father. The San Francisco clinic couldn't have had access to his DNA. He hadn't been to California in years.

Unless—

With an intake of breath, Alex remembered his visit to a Swiss medical clinic, early in his marriage, when he'd still hoped for a child and had wondered why they hadn't conceived. He'd gone to get tested for problems, and agreed to let them keep the samples for the future, just in case. Could it possibly be—

His lips parted.

Yes, he realized. It could. His dead wife, so clever and ruthless, must have known he'd demand a paternity test. The baby would have to be provably his; blackmail would never work otherwise. She could have bribed her way to getting his sample from the Swiss clinic, and had it sent to San Francisco.

The thought was chilling. Had Chiara found a way to take her revenge, even from beyond the grave?

Could it really be possible that Rosalie Brown, a woman he'd never met before today, was pregnant with his baby?

CHAPTER TWO

"ARE THEY STILL HERE? Why won't they leave?" Rosalie's wizened great-aunt whispered in French as she stood in the kitchen doorway, staring at the tourists singing on the other side of her restaurant. Looking at Rosalie, she scowled, putting her hand on her hip beneath her frilly apron. "And for the last time, stop smiling! It's enough to curdle the eggs!"

"I'm sorry—I can't help it." But it wasn't just the singing tourists who were making Rosalie smile. The truth was, since she'd arrived at Mont-Saint-Michel two days ago, she'd barely stopped grinning.

Her baby was hers.

Well and truly hers. When she'd left San Francisco for Venice, she'd thought it an impossible dream.

But that dream had actually come true. Rosalie could keep her baby. Her child was hers alone. Now and forever.

Joy lit up her heart. Standing by an empty

table, she did an impromptu little dance, hugging her huge belly.

We're a family, baby. You and me.

And she felt her unborn baby dance with her, turning over, kicking his joy.

"Do not dance in the middle of my restaurant!" Great-aunt Odette looked scandalized. "You are acting as drunk as the tourists!"

"Drunk on happiness, *Tatie*," Rosalie replied fondly, giving her a big kiss on the cheek. Her white-haired great-aunt pulled away, wiping her cheek.

"My sister never should have moved to America. You do not know how to behave! You are embarrassing yourself!"

But her words had no sting. In spite of her bluster, her aunt was hiding a smile. For about the hundredth time, Rosalie was glad she'd had a few extra days before her scheduled return flight to California. Since getting custody of her baby had been so unexpectedly fast and easy, she'd taken the train from Venice to see her great-aunt in France. Odette Lancel owned the most popular omelet restaurant on the tiny island of Mont-Saint-Michel, in the village beneath the medieval abbey, clinging to the rock jutting from the sea.

Not that Grande-tante Odette had been happy at first to see her only relative show up on her doorstep, unmarried and heavily pregnant. That first day had been filled with many French scoldings which, fortunately, Rosalie had been too happy to take to heart. But Odette Lancel had made it clear she thought her young great-niece exceedingly silly to have gotten pregnant via surrogacy, and even more naive to now plan to raise the baby alone.

"A baby needs two parents, ma petite," Odette had told her firmly. "And as foolish a child as you obviously are, I know you had a happy childhood. Your mother was a dear creature, and I know you loved your father. And they loved you..."

At the mention of her parents, Rosalie's joy had briefly dimmed. She couldn't bear to remember her wonderful parents who had died, and the happiness of her childhood home, all lost forever. Because of her.

And Chiara Falconeri, too, had died. Rosalie had met the beautiful, chic Italian woman only briefly in San Francisco. Such a tragedy, dying so suddenly. And apparently her marriage, far from being happy, had in truth been a misery. She'd died with her lover, cheating on her husband. After she'd created the child without Alex Falconeri's consent—trying to force him into a divorce?

It was all so messed up. Rosalie was grateful and relieved she'd raise her baby away from all that, in a home that would be filled with love, not drama.

"A boy needs a father," her great-aunt had insisted.

"It's impossible," Rosalie replied with equal firmness. "The father of my baby is..."

Handsome. Darkly sexy. Powerful.

Images of Alex Falconeri flooded through her.

Resolutely, she pushed away the memory, finishing, "He's newly bereaved and not interested in raising a child."

"Still, he has responsibilities."

"I don't want his money," Rosalie replied, annoyed.

"Why?" Her great-aunt's dark eyes narrowed. "As a receptionist, do you make such a fortune?"

"No," Rosalie had admitted, then added reluctantly, "I have my parents' life insurance. And if I sell my family's land..."

"Sell your land?" Odette had been scandalized. "I never approved of my niece marrying an American farmer, but she spoke of the land with pride. Your father's family farmed it for generations. Just as this restaurant was started by my grandpère." She'd looked around the bustling tables of L'Omeletterie. "One should not cast aside a family legacy lightly."

"Of course I wouldn't. I'm not." A lump lifted in Rosalie's throat. "But—the farm's gone, Tatie*. My parents are dead. I can never go back. I must accept that."*

Her great-aunt's voice had trembled. "Rosalie—"

"I only have a few days before I go back to California. Why don't I help you in the restaurant?"

Rosalie couldn't have chosen a better way to distract Odette. Her great-aunt's face had lit up, for the busy tourist season was in full swing. And so Rosalie had spent the last two days clearing up dishes and chatting with customers in English and French.

She was almost regretful that today would be her last day, since tomorrow she must return to Venice, and take her ticketed flight back to San Francisco.

Then decisions would need to be made. Because she obviously could not raise a crying baby in a tiny two-bedroom apartment with three roommates. And could Rosalie really keep working as a receptionist after her baby was born, when the cost of childcare would be more than her actual salary?

Her parents' life insurance was not much, and would not last, even if she felt comfortable about spending it, which she didn't. But could she really sell her family's acres to the highest bidder?

As the tourists joyfully screeched their song about baseball across the restaurant, Rosalie blinked, relieved to be pulled from her thoughts. It was late, and all the tables had become empty but one. A group of rowdy American tourists was cheering and drunkenly singing, their arms looped around each other's shoulders. Their beloved team had soundly beaten some bitter rival. They were all gray haired and well past middle age, but their joie de vivre and energy was greater than most college students had. Watching them from across the restaurant, Rosalie couldn't stop smiling, no matter what her aunt said.

"Make them stop, *ma petite*," Odette whispered to her in French, her wrinkled face irritated.

"Why?" Rosalie gave a low laugh, looking around the darkened restaurant. The day-trippers from Paris had already departed on the last shuttle, leaving the island quiet, with only a few tourists remaining. The hotels on Mont-Saint-Michel were tiny, with just a few hotel rooms scattered across the steep island. "There's no one left here to bother."

"They're bothering *me*." Her great-aunt gave an expressive sniff. "It's past ten. The good heaven knows they should be headed to their beds. Do they expect me to cart them up the hill in a wheelbarrow?"

"I'll tell them to leave."

"Good."

But going over to the rowdy table, Rosalie impulsively joined them in the chorus, causing the tourists to shout their appreciation.

"Congratulations on your game, guys," she said in English.

"You're American," one of the women exclaimed. "What are you doing in Mont-Saint-Michel?"

"My great-aunt owns this restaurant." Taking the empty glasses of kir Normands and putting them on her tray, Rosalie gently set down the bill.

"I've never had such a good omelet!" a man said, patting his belly.

"I can see why they're so famous," another chimed in. "Thirty euros, but worth it!"

"How do you make them so fluffy?" a woman begged.

Rosalie leaned forward confidentially. "I'm not supposed to share this." Her great-aunt, watching from the doorway, rolled her eyes. She'd seen this before. Rosalie continued, "It's a family secret, but maybe I'll share it. Just this once." The entire table waited, rapt and breathless. She whispered, "It's love."

The tourists sat back in their chairs, groaning.

Rosalie grinned. In answer to their good-natured complaining, she replied firmly, "I'm serious. That's how everything truly special is created in this world. Love."

And she had to believe that. Sometimes life seemed like one heartbreak after another—but love existed. It was love that gave meaning and magic to everything.

And it worked in mysterious ways. How else to explain that, in her darkest hour, filled with grief and despair, she'd become pregnant—she, who'd never even slept with a man before? How else to explain the miracle that she could keep her baby?

Rosalie knew how lucky she was. She had to fiercely cherish every drop of joy. She wrapped one hand around her baby bump. This was more than a drop. This was an ocean.

She didn't understand why Alex Falconeri had been willing to abandon his own child, but whatever the reason, she would be grateful to him for the rest of her life.

But even as she had the thought, she heard a husky voice.

"Miss Brown."

Frowning, she straightened, glancing behind her. Then her lips parted in a silent gasp.

Alex Falconeri stood in the restaurant's doorway, his broad shoulders blocking the light from the hallway entrance. His handsome face, half-shadowed in silhouette, was wreathed in a scowl.

Her body went weak. Trembling, she set down her tray.

"Thank you again. We'll tell all our friends about this place," the Americans said, and tossing money down on the table for the bill, they wobbled to their feet and wavered happily and drunkenly out of the restaurant.

But Rosalie barely heard them. She stared at the darkly charismatic man that she thought she'd left behind forever.

"Miss Brown," he said again, his voice low and

husky. The vibrations curled around her like mist, and she swallowed, her teeth suddenly chattering.

"H-how did you f-find me here? What do you want?"

He blended with the shadows in his dark gray shirt and black trousers and long dark coat. "It was not difficult to find you. I called a few hours ago and spoke with your aunt."

"My—" She whirled around accusingly at Odette, who was scooping all the piles of euros from the table into her apron.

The elderly lady drew herself up haughtily to her full five feet. "He is the father. As I told you, he has a responsibility, *non*?"

"No," Rosalie informed her, then turned and glared at him. "You verbally terminated your parental rights in Venice."

Alex's eyebrows rose. "Is that what you think?" he said incredulously. "You just show up out of the blue and tell me some ridiculous story, and when I don't immediately believe it, you think I terminated all my rights to my child?"

Yes. That was exactly what Rosalie had thought. Her heart fell to the floor, and her knees trembled. She leaned against the table.

There was only one reason he could be here: he wanted to take her baby from her after all. And he could. With all his money and power, who could stop him?

"Please," she whispered. "Just leave me alone."

Alex Falconeri started to speak, then hesitated, glancing at her great-aunt. Narrowing his eyes, he turned back to Rosalie.

"Come with me."

Mont-Saint-Michel's tiny cobblestoned street, dark beneath the moonlight, was empty except for the departing group of American tourists.

Alex looked at Rosalie Brown, who was dressed as a waitress in a simple black shift dress and white apron. She looked angry—and terrified.

"Goodbye!" one of the tourists called back to her, waving. Rosalie didn't respond.

Alex set his jaw. He hardly wanted a bunch of strangers to hear what he had to say to her. Just as he hadn't relished having her great-aunt listening in, looking as if she was memorizing every word to repeat to a lawyer later.

"This way," he told Rosalie grimly, leading her up the nearest flight of steps. It led to the high stone rampart that surrounded the steeply vertical island. Up on the ramparts, all was quiet, except the wind and seagulls. Mont-Saint-Michel, which had once been a fortress, a monastery and a prison, seemed haunted beneath the moonlight, as it overlooked the shadowed beauty of the bay.

But it was when Alex turned back to look at Rosalie that he truly caught his breath.

Standing next to him, she looked up at him

with big dark eyes that seemed to echo with ripples of moonlight, like the tide. A cool wind blew her hair, and she was biting her deliciously full lower lip. Beneath her white apron, her simple black dress showed off her full breasts and belly swelling with his child.

His child.

Alex still couldn't believe it.

After she'd left his palazzo in Venice two days ago, he'd called a private investigator, the best and most expensive. Yesterday, Alex had called the fertility clinic in San Francisco and interviewed them at length. Now he knew everything.

But he hadn't just confirmed her story. He'd learned everything about Rosalie Brown—oh, yes—from the grades she'd gotten in her rural school to the recent tragic deaths of her parents in a wildfire.

Odette Lancel was her only remaining family. It hadn't taken a genius to track Rosalie to Mont-Saint-Michel.

Which was good, because the last thing Alex felt like at the moment was a genius.

He could hardly believe the depths of his dead wife's betrayal. Or her determination to gain the upper hand. And she would have. If not for her sudden, shocking death, she would have gotten what she wanted. Because she'd found the one thing more important to him than his honor. More important than his fortune.

"Why did you come here?" Rosalie's voice was low. "In Venice you called me a liar and said I couldn't possibly be pregnant with your child."

"I was wrong."

She gave a bitter laugh. "Thank you." She looked away. "What did you tell my aunt? That you wanted to share custody?"

"Not exactly." As he looked at the beautiful girl standing on the haunted stone parapet, he thought she looked like a lost princess in a medieval fairy tale.

Obviously the shocking events of the last month were starting to take a toll on Alex. Because there was no such thing as magic. Fairy tales weren't real, and this girl, however beautiful she might be, didn't need a knight to save her. She was a young woman who'd agreed to bear a child for money.

But why? Knowing what he knew about her, money was the last thing Rosalie Brown needed. She had received multiple offers on valuable farmland in Sonoma County, famous for its vineyards. She could have sold it. Failing that, she could have asked him for a small fortune in Venice two days before. But she hadn't.

He knew everything, but he understood nothing.

"What do you want, then?" Rosalie demanded.

"I've had you investigated," he said slowly. "I've learned everything about you. But there are things I don't understand."

"Investigated?" She turned pale. "You had no right to invade my privacy—"

"Why did you agree to get pregnant by a stranger and give away the baby at birth? Was it really for the money?"

Her eyes flashed. "It was a mistake. I never should have agreed to be a surrogate."

"Why did you?"

"I thought," her voice faltered, "I could do something good in the world, something that would make up for… Well." Her jaw set. "I made a mistake when I signed the surrogacy contract. I changed my mind almost at once, but…by then it was too late."

"You were already pregnant."

She gave a single nod.

"How could you believe Chiara with her ridiculous story? Did you really believe that any man would be *too busy* to meet the future mother of his child?"

She suddenly couldn't meet his gaze. "That isn't actually what she said."

"What did she say?"

"She said…um…"

"What?"

Rosalie lifted her chin. "That you were impotent."

Alex stared at her, his mouth open.

Then he burst into a laugh. He laughed until the girl's defiant glare changed to bewilderment, then concern. As if she thought he'd suddenly gone mad.

And maybe he had. He thought of the years he'd put up with his wife's affair. The years he'd told himself she would eventually come to her senses and return to their marriage. How he'd convinced himself he could forgive her and take her back, when she would be chastened by experience, wiser, ready to finally become a decent partner and eventually, a good mother to their children.

Impotent.

It was almost amusing, how childish and vengeful she'd been, in her frustration at not getting her way. His lips quirked as he shook his head.

"I didn't particularly enjoy having sex with her, but I wasn't impotent."

Her cheeks turned red. "No?"

"We weren't close, and yes, she seemed cold, but I thought that meant she'd be a steady, practical partner for building a business and a family. When she didn't get pregnant after a few months, I went to a clinic in Switzerland to get tested. The doctors saw no problem." He paused. "Later I discovered she'd been on the Pill the whole time."

Rosalie's eyes widened. "She lied to you?"

"She'd only married me to please her father. As soon as he was dead and she safely had her inheritance, she was desperate to be free." He paused. "Chiara bribed a technician in California to forge documents and get my sample from the Swiss clinic."

"Just to get a divorce?"

"To hold me hostage," he said softly. "She meant to tell me I had a child, then hide him away from me, until I gave her what she wanted. Not just a divorce. She also wanted me to tear up our prenuptial agreement. She wanted to keep all her own money, but also take half of mine. It was the only way her lover said he'd marry her. If she could keep him in Ferraris and cocaine for the rest of his life."

Rosalie's eyes went big. "What kind of people marry for reasons like that?"

"Why else would anyone marry, except for financial reasons, or to create a home for children?"

"For—for love," she stammered. "That's the only reason. Isn't it? True love that lasts forever?"

He stared at her. "Do you feel that way about sex?"

Her blush deepened, and she suddenly couldn't meet his eyes. "Or course," she mumbled. "Love is the basis of everything. Or it should be."

"You're quite a romantic," he said finally.

"You say that like it's a bad thing."

Because it was. Alex drew closer to her in the moonlight. Standing by the rough-hewn parapets overlooking the sea, he heard the rush of the tide, the roar of the wind and the cries of seagulls overhead. He had that strange feeling again, like they were alone together in some strange fantasy world. "I don't understand. If love is so important to you, why would you agree to have a child for money?"

"Not for money. For love." Her voice caught. "I thought I could bring another family together, to try to make up for what happened to—" She suddenly shook her head, her eyes shimmering with tears. "Why didn't your wife just get pregnant herself?" she choked out. "Why drag me into your fight?"

"Chiara didn't want to be biologically related to the child. Apparently, not even she—" he looked at Rosalie "—could imagine abandoning her own baby."

She stared at him for a moment, and then he saw the moment his barb hit. Her nostrils flared.

"Well, I'm not abandoning this baby now. Not to you. Not to anyone." Rosalie hugged her belly over the black shift dress and white apron. "He's mine."

Alex decided to test her one last time. "Is there any amount of money I could pay you to give up the child? What is your price, Miss Brown? How much would it take for you to give me my son and disappear from our lives?"

"There is no amount!"

"A million euros? Ten?"

"No! Leave us alone!" she cried and whirled away. He grabbed her wrist.

"I can't let you go."

"You can't force me to stay." She wrenched her wrist from his grasp. "Surrogacy is illegal in Italy."

His eyes tightened. "You're right. Surrogacy with no biological connection is illegal in my home country." As he saw her exhale, he continued smoothly, "But that's not relevant in this case. You are the mother, Miss Brown, and I am the father—it's as simple as that. I have rights. I will not let you go."

"I will die before I leave my baby to be raised in that *museum*, with a father who has ice for a heart!"

Alex let her insult of his family home pass without comment, but— "Ice?"

She glared at him. "Your wife was desperate to be free of you. Desperate! Why couldn't you face reality? Why couldn't you just let her go?" Her eyes glittered. "If you'd just given her what she wanted, I wouldn't have been dragged into it. I thought I was doing something good in the world—something that would make another family happy, and that I'd feel…something…other than—"

Her voice choked off as she looked away.

Alex remembered what the investigator had told him about her parents' deaths. They'd died last autumn, just weeks before the girl had contacted the fertility clinic. There had been horrifying pictures of burned fields, her childhood home razed to the foundations. An entire farm village in Northern California had been lost by the raging fire. Sixty people had died, including Ernst and Mireille Brown.

Could that be why the girl had agreed to the surrogacy? Could she really be such an idealist—believing in *true love*, trying to save others to heal her own pain?

"You lost your parents," he said slowly. Her shoulders snapped back.

"I don't want to talk about it."

He came closer. "Your parents had just died in a fire. You felt sad and alone. So you decided to help strangers have a baby."

He saw her swallow, furiously blinking back tears. She looked away. "My mother used to say that if I was feeling sad, I should try to make someone else's life better, and maybe it would make my life a little better too." She looked up at him, and he saw the heartbreak in her beautiful face. "Then I realized what a mistake I'd made, thinking I could ever give up my baby. So I went to Venice. That's when the miracle happened."

"You discovered Chiara was dead."

She looked at him, her expression horrified. "No! Whatever she might have done, her death was a tragedy." She took a deep breath. "The miracle was when you said you didn't want my baby. When you accused me of lying and told me to get the hell out. Those were the sweetest words I'd ever heard in my life. Like angels singing."

Her words were so ludicrous they almost made him smile. His cursing had sounded like a choir of angels?

"But there are no miracles." Her voice cracked as she looked up at the highest spire of the thousand-year-old abbey crowning the island. "Just tragedy."

Alex stared at her. Up here on the ramparts with the wind blowing, he could taste the salt of the sea like tears.

When he'd first met Rosalie Brown, he'd imagined her to be like Chiara. She wasn't. He saw that now. She was a do-gooder, romantic and naive. She'd tried to channel her grief into making the world a better place.

It had been a long time since he'd met anyone so unselfish. Certainly not since his sister, Margaret, had died. No wonder he hadn't recognized it at first.

"Perhaps," he said slowly, "we can raise the baby together."

"Together?" He saw the flash of longing in her eyes, then dismay. She clearly wanted to be with her baby, but however much his opinion of her had improved, her opinion of *him* was obviously more dismal than ever.

Usually, he didn't care what people thought. But for some reason, in this case he did. "Why not?"

"How? I live in California."

"Not anymore. You will live with me in Italy until the baby is born. And after I get a DNA test, you will remain. Forever."

"What are you saying?" she whispered. She wiped a trembling hand over her eyes. "You—you want to marry me?"

He barked a laugh, which echoed across the ramparts. It was only when he saw her flinch that he bit it back. "Forgive me. But marry? No." He snorted. "I was married once. Never again."

"Then—" Rosalie blinked, confused. "I don't understand. What exactly are you suggesting?"

Alex lifted a dark eyebrow. "You will live with me. I will provide for you. I'll give you an allowance, more than you can possibly spend—"

"I'm not a gold digger! I'm not interested in your money!"

"Fine," he said, annoyed. Then he had a sudden idea. He gave her a grin. "As you wish. You can get a job and pay your own way, every step. You'll come to Venice and live with us." He tilted his head. "As the nanny."

CHAPTER THREE

ROSALIE STARED AT him in shock. Then she lost it.

"The *nanny*?" she screeched.

"Is that a problem?" Alex replied.

She put her hands protectively over her belly. "I'm his *mother*. Not some employee!"

"A few days ago, you were just a hired womb. I'd think becoming the baby's nanny would feel like a promotion."

"Are you drunk?" she demanded. "You must be, if you think I'd ever agree to be my own child's nanny!"

Alex looked her over slowly, at her black shift dress and waitress's white apron. "Am I correct in believing you are not in possession of a trust fund? That you have no..." he paused "...*private estate*?"

Rosalie thought of her family's thousand-acre farm as it had been, and the warm golden patina on the hundred-year-old Victorian house she'd grown up in. Then she blinked, remembering it as it was now, nothing but a thousand acres of charred ash. She'd only looked at it for a millisecond, on the way to the funeral, but it would forever be burned into her mind.

Swallowing hard, she focused on Alex. He was looking at her strangely.

"No trust fund," she said shortly. She didn't mention her parents' life insurance, because it made her feel sick to think of it, and anyway it wasn't very much. "Just a job in San Francisco. Where I'm expected on Monday."

"I see." His sensual lips curved. "But since you've made it clear you won't accept any handouts from me, you will need to earn money somehow while you're living in Italy, will you not?"

"I haven't said I'm moving to Italy, but if I did, I'd get an actual job—"

"It can be difficult for an American to get a job in the European Union without a work permit. Unless, perhaps, you are highly skilled in some technical field?"

She thought of her job answering phones for a seafood wholesaler on the Embarcadero. "No," she said tightly.

"You perhaps have the capital to start a business that will create jobs for Italian workers?"

Not without selling her land. Which she couldn't. Not yet. Maybe not ever. "No."

"Do you speak Italian?"

"No," she whispered.

He changed tactics. "Well, let's say, for the sake

of argument, you still found a full-time job. Then you'd spend all your daytime hours away from our newborn son, and that would defeat the whole reason for you moving to Italy, would it not?"

Rosalie stared at him, feeling dizzy. His words were spinning her in circles, making her doubt herself, making her actually wonder if his argument was reasonable. "I haven't said I will live with you."

"Or here's another idea." He looked at her sideways. "You could simply allow me to support you."

"No," she cried. "I don't want your money!"

He shrugged. "Then—nanny it is," he said lightly. "It is a compromise. A way for us to raise our son in Italy together."

"Funny compromise. It seems I'm the only one making any sacrifices here, quitting my job and moving around the world."

Alex looked at her. "Would you really be giving up so much by leaving San Francisco?"

Rosalie thought of what waited for her there. A job where she felt anonymous to her bosses and was screamed at by customers. A tattered two-bedroom apartment with a revolving door of roommates who worked long hours to pay the rent, and went out clubbing and brought home men whenever they weren't. She'd even found herself locked out of her own bedroom and forced to sleep on the lumpy sofa, whenever her roommate brought home one-night stands.

But even *that* was preferable to going home to Emmetsville.

So sell, a voice whispered inside her. *Just sell the farm and you'll never have to see it again.*

The land was in wine country between Sonoma and Petaluma. She'd already received multiple offers, each more shockingly high than the last. With that much in her bank account, she could wipe that smug look off Alex's face in an instant. The nanny, indeed.

"The truth is," Alex said quietly, "You don't have any desire to return to San Francisco."

It was as if he was reading her mind. "Why do you say that?"

"Because if you enjoyed living in San Francisco, you'd have already sold the land you inherited from your parents in Sonoma County."

She stared at him in shock.

"I told you—I know everything," he said. "You could have sold the land to one of the big wineries and changed your life. Plenty of money to buy a fancy condo or get a college degree or take a luxury cruise around the world. But you haven't done any of those things."

She looked away. "No."

He shook his head. "You can't bring yourself to sell the land. But you can't bring yourself to go back to it, either. You're stuck. A detail that was made obvious to me when you didn't bring up the fact that you are, in fact, in possession of a large fortune. Just one you do not wish to spend." He looked at her. "Well?"

Rosalie's heart was pounding wildly. She looked longingly at the steps that led down to the cobblestoned lane, and the safety of her great-aunt's restaurant.

"I want you to come and live with me, Rosalie. You are the mother of my child. Let me support you." He gave a small smile. "As your aunt pointed out, it is my responsibility."

"No one gives something for nothing," she whispered. She didn't want to owe him anything. She took a deep breath. "Maybe I could be a nanny."

Alex blinked, looking surprised. "As you wish," he said softly. "You'll spend your days caring for our baby, exactly as you wish, without having to worry about your financial security, and knowing you have a safety net if I ever fire you…"

"*Fire* me?"

"Yes. We'll draw up a contract. You'll have severance, so there would be nothing to worry about. Or if you grow tired of motherhood, and leave us—"

"Are you crazy?"

"You'll still have all the benefits of an employment contract. And be protected."

Rosalie's only experience with a contract had been the disastrous one with the fertility clinic. That hadn't made her eager to sign another one. "Protected? From what?"

Pressing his lips together tightly, he didn't answer.

Rosalie repeated in a hard voice, "Protected from what, Alex?"

He said abruptly, "From me."

Her mouth went dry. "Why—why would I need protecting from you?"

Alex came closer to her and her heart quickened as his powerful body stopped just inches from hers, his hard, handsome face half hidden in shadow.

"Because I might be tempted to seduce you," he said softly.

Her lips parted as a shiver went over her body. "What?"

"Having you living in my house, when you're not just so beautiful, but also the mother of my child…"

"You think I'm beautiful?" Rosalie felt dizzy.

His eyes fell briefly to her mouth, then lifted back up. "It would perhaps help us to draw clear boundaries. So there's no danger."

"Danger," she echoed. She felt it. Something about being close to him did strange things to her, body and soul.

Why? Because he was so darkly handsome?

So rich and powerful? So sensual and wicked, with his cruel lips and husky voice, with its barest hint of Italian accent?

All that, and she was pregnant with his baby. It would be astonishing if she *didn't* feel shivery every time he was near.

But she couldn't believe he would call her beautiful. Even if she weren't heavily pregnant, she wouldn't be remotely in his league. His type of woman would be obviously more like Chiara—chic, pin thin, wickedly gorgeous, devastatingly clever.

While Rosalie was just an ordinary girl in a shapeless dress and waitress apron, who wore her heart on her sleeve. Of petite height and tending toward plumpness, she'd never cared much about fashion, either. She bought her clothes at the discount superstore and used coupons whenever she could.

She looked at Alex Falconeri. Whatever he might say about being tempted, there was no way *he* could be worried about losing control and seducing her.

There was only one explanation.

He'd seen how attracted Rosalie was to him, and was trying to let her down easy. How could he not see the impact he had on her, when her cheeks went red and her body trembled whenever he got close, whenever he even *looked* at her?

Gorgeous as he was, and a wealthy Italian

count too, this type of thing probably happened to him all the time. Obviously, he was politely trying to warn her off.

Who could blame him when she'd just practically blurted out a marriage proposal? Her cheeks burned.

"So." He looked down at her. "You wish to be the nanny?"

She stared at him, then stubbornly shook her head. "I don't want to be your employee."

"You won't let me support you, you won't let me hire you—" Muttering in Italian, Alex rubbed the back of his head, looking as irritated as a man that handsome and suave *could* look, when he had the face of a dark angel. He bit out, "So what is the solution?"

Taking a deep breath, Rosalie said, "How about I keep my job in San Francisco, take two months' maternity leave, and we both chip in together and get a studio apartment there? Or if you prefer, you could get your own place, and I'll let you visit the baby. Whenever you want," she added generously.

Alex stared at her for a moment, then he snorted. "You've got guts. I'll give you that."

"I was just thinking the same about you." She paused. "*Guts* is such an American word. And you barely have an accent."

"My mother was American," he said coldly. "Like you."

"Oh, was she?" Rosalie opened her eyes wide

in mock surprise. "*Your* mom was a farm girl who once took second place at the county fair for her pie crust? Or maybe you mean—" she tilted her head "—she, too, worked as a receptionist for minimum wage, and volunteered for Meals on Wheels in high school?"

His lips curved slightly as he considered her. "My mother was a debutante. A Cabot from Boston who attended Wellesley."

"Of course," Rosalie said, barely resisting the urge to roll her eyes. "*Exactly* like me."

She'd had enough. Turning on her heel, she started down the steep stone steps from the rampart, back into the little village behind the walls.

"Where are you going?" he demanded. "Nothing is decided—"

"Wrong." She looked back at him. "I've decided I'm going to bed. And don't worry, that wasn't an invitation."

"Rosalie—"

"Good night," she said firmly.

She went carefully down the steps back into the village, then went more quickly up the lane toward her great-aunt's door. Away from his presence, she felt like she could breathe again.

But as she reached the restaurant, Alex was suddenly beside her. He'd easily caught up to her with his long strides.

"I told you, you're not invited," she said uneasily. His sensual lips curved.

"I'm coming to help you pack."

"I'm not going to Venice with you."

"Oh, yes, you are," Odette said in French behind her. Turning, Rosalie saw her tiny, hunched great-aunt glaring from the doorway.

"Excuse me," she bit out to Alex, then stomped inside the restaurant, closing the door firmly behind her.

"You don't understand," she argued.

"I understand perfectly," Odette countered. "The father of your baby would like you to live with him, to get to know you, and help raise the child he never knew about. Alex Falconeri is handling this like a gentleman."

"A gentleman—are you crazy? He's bullying me into living with him in Venice! In his palace!" Even Rosalie was aware of how ridiculous a complaint this must sound. Scowling, she felt herself on firmer ground as she argued, "He wanted to hire me as my own baby's *nanny*!"

"You refused, of course."

"Of course I did. I'm his son's mother, not his employee."

The elderly lady snorted. "As far as men are concerned, they don't often see any difference," she said tartly, then added, "You must get to know each other. Then, perhaps, for the child's sake, you will decide to marry."

Rosalie's cheeks burned. "I already suggested that."

"*Mon Dieu*, you are a fast worker."

"It was a misunderstanding, that's all. But he shot down the idea. He was married once already, and he takes his vows seriously. Perhaps a little too seriously," she added, thinking about all the problems this had caused.

Odette regarded her with bright eyes. "A man who takes his vows too seriously? There is no such thing."

"But *Tatie*—"

"You will give him a chance. The baby is his as much as it is yours. Does the child not deserve to have more family?"

"The baby has me. And you," Rosalie said desperately. Her great-aunt smiled.

"*Ma petite*, I will not live forever. And a boy needs a father."

"But it's not right—why should I go live with him in Italy? I don't know anyone there."

"Is there so much for you back in California?"

Rosalie thought of her childhood home, burned to ash. And her parents, who'd died in the fire, and it was her fault, all her fault. If she'd married the boy next door like they'd wanted, she would have been there to save them. She would have known to get them out before it was too late.

All that she had waiting for her in California was ash and regret.

So what if she went to Italy with her baby's father? What if, at least for a while, she agreed to live in his palazzo?

“But I don’t want to be the nanny,” she said in a small voice.

“Of course you do not,” her great-aunt sniffed. “You are pregnant with a rich man’s child. You will allow him to pay for everything.”

Rosalie stared at her. “I couldn’t!”

“Why?”

“It would be…charity! And my father always said, *No one gets something for nothing.*”

“Something for nothing indeed.” Odette snorted. “You are pregnant with his baby, Rosalie, creating the child in your body. You will go through hard, painful labor to give birth. Then you will be up night and day, nursing the baby, rocking him to sleep, boiling bottles and so forth.” Odette, who was childless, waved her hand vaguely. “If that is not work, what is? If anything, *he* is the one accepting charity from you. After all, what is he doing to help with all these tasks? Nothing! But nothing!”

Rosalie stared at her great-aunt. “You are crazy.” But she suddenly leaned over and gave the wrinkled cheek a fierce kiss.

“You are welcome.” Odette gave a satisfied nod. “That is why young people need the older ones. To tell you about life.”

Taking off her apron, Rosalie hung it up on a

hook and went back outside to where Alex waited, a hulking shadowy figure in the moonlight.

"I've decided I'll come with you."

His expression didn't change, but his shoulders relaxed. *"Va bene."*

"Just for a little while. Just so we can get to know each other."

"I will convince you to stay."

"Not as your nanny," she countered. "Since I'm agreeing to move to your city, you will pay for everything, food, housing, medical care. Even a stipend for extra expenses while I'm living in Venice."

"Yes," he said instantly.

She was astonished at how quickly he agreed. "And once the baby is born and you have your paternity test, you will always pay child support. Whether we live in the same house or not."

"Of course." Alex tilted his head. "Anything else?"

Rosalie thought fast. "And you must promise, if us living together doesn't work out for whatever reason, you will not try to bully me into giving you full custody."

"As long as you agree to the same."

She nearly choked a laugh, that Alex Falconeri, the wealthy, powerful Conte di Rialto, would think *she* could bully *him* into anything. But her smile faded as she looked at his face. She stuck out her hand. "Agreed."

"Agreed." He took her hand in his.

As his larger hand enfolded hers, she felt the warmth and roughness of his palm. His fingers pressed between hers, pushing down against her own. Electricity coursed through her body, making her breasts heavy and nipples taut.

Alex abruptly pulled his hand away.

She exhaled. Had she done it again? Revealed her pathetic desire, embarrassing herself and making him uncomfortable?

His handsome face was inscrutable.

Cheeks hot, she turned, muttering, "I'll go pack."

He was suddenly there beside her. "I'm coming too."

"Why?" She could barely bring herself to look at him. She tried to joke, "Are you afraid I might try to climb out the window?"

"The thought had crossed my mind."

"You obviously haven't seen the window. But fine, do what you want."

Inside the empty restaurant, Rosalie led him up the stairs in the back, then up another flight, and another flight still, each set of stairs more slender and vertical than the last. At the last flight, he frowned. "Are you sure this is safe for you? I can go get your things, if you tell me where they are."

Alex was being protective of her? For a moment she was touched and surprised. Then she realized it was his baby he was worried about, not her. Falling down a flight of stairs two months before her due date might lead to an onset of early labor. "I'm fine," she said stubbornly. "I've done this tons of times over the last two days. Come on."

At the very top was the tiny garret of her aunt's small hotel, an attic room far too undesirable for any paying guest.

Rosalie switched on a small lamp, which cast a soft glow on the slanted walls, barely reaching into the shadows. A single lonely bed was stuffed against the slanted wall next to a bare clothing rack. Leaning awkwardly, she pulled her overnight bag from beneath the bed, then swiftly packed it with her few items of clothes, blushing when she packed her extra bra and underwear over her rumpled paperback copy of *Murder on the Orient Express*.

Coming into the room behind her, he made no comment. Because of the slanted roof, he could only stand up straight in the middle of the room. Just having him so close to her made her feel a flash of heat across her skin.

Taking a deep breath, she glanced out the window, which she'd pushed open earlier for fresh air in the stuffy room. Trying to calm her heart, she looked at the tiny village clinging to the rock beneath her, and beyond the ramparts, the moonlit sea. In the distance, she heard a seagull's plaintive cry, like a lost soul searching, searching, searching and never finding.

"Alex—" Turning abruptly in the tight space of the room, she was suddenly pushed up against him.

"Yes?" He looked down at her. It was just the two of them alone beside a single bed.

Her whole body flushed hot beneath her black shift dress. Awkwardly, she turned away, yanking the sheets off the tiny bed. "I just need to drop these in the laundry room."

"Allow me." As he took her bag, then the sheets and blankets, his fingertips brushed hers. She swallowed.

What was wrong with her? Why was he having this effect on her? She'd never felt this way before about anyone. Certainly not Cody, the one time he'd tried to kiss her on that disastrous date, or any of the men she'd met in San Francisco, or the boys from high school. Was it pregnancy hormones?

Or was it just the fact that Alex Falconeri was the most obscenely sexy man she'd ever met?

Pushing past him, she fled the tiny garret. After going back down the stairs, she led him to the laundry room, then to the bathroom she'd shared with her aunt. Gathering up a small toiletry bag, she tucked it into the overnight bag still on his shoulder, then paused, knowing she should take the bag and carry it herself. She carried her own burdens, always.

But as she started to reach for the straps, she remembered her aunt's stern admonition. Okay. She was seven months' pregnant. Maybe she could accept help. But it wasn't easy.

Clenching her hands at her sides so she wouldn't be tempted to take the bag, she faced him with all the dignity she could muster. "I'm ready."

Rosalie just prayed he couldn't see the impact he was having on her. If he did…it would be even more embarrassing than when she'd blurted out the question asking if he was proposing to her. She could only imagine how humiliated she'd feel if he felt he had to explicitly tell her he wasn't interested in her physically. Again.

From now on, she told herself firmly as they headed downstairs, she would focus on one job. And it might be the most difficult job she'd ever had.

She would stop wanting Alex Falconeri.

CHAPTER FOUR

ALEX'S BLOOD WAS pumping as he watched Rosalie hug her great-aunt farewell. He'd gotten what he wanted. She was returning to live with him in Venice.

He didn't begrudge the deal they'd made. A stipend? Negligible. Child support? Obviously. Custody? He was relieved they'd promised not to battle each other with underhanded tricks. Yes, he had far more money for a protracted custody fight, but courts tended to be swayed with sympathy for a loving mother. And Rosalie's love for her unborn child was clear.

As was her incredible charisma. Her petite, curvy frame, her luminous brown eyes, so soulful and alive, her plump lips, her dark hair with streaks of sunlight around her heart-shaped face—

No judge alive could resist a plea from a woman like this, and a jury even less so. Any case Alex took to court against her, he would lose.

He would have paid any price to get her to willingly move to his palazzo in Venice. He could not easily have moved to California for a multitude of reasons. His vineyard was one. His inability to get on a plane was another. He was relieved she'd given in, and was going to let him support her. He'd only suggested Rosalie become a nanny because she'd been so strangely reluctant to let him pay her way. What did he care about money? He was glad to support both her and the child. *Of course* he should support them.

But he hadn't lied about wanting to create firm boundaries. Making her his employee would have helped with that. But now, there was nothing to prevent him from acting on his desire and making her his mistress. He'd be living in the same house with her. Wanting her with this ravenous hunger.

But he could never allow himself to have her.

Because a woman like Rosalie Brown only wanted true love. She'd said so. For her, it was the only reason for marriage, the only reason for sex.

Love is the basis of everything. Or it should be.

She'd been raised in a loving home. She actually believed that was *normal*. It was why she'd become a surrogate. To bring another family together, to try to heal her own grief over the parents she'd lost. For love, all for love.

While Alex had no love to give.

Just learning to be a father would be hard enough. He sucked in his breath.

All this time, he'd wanted a child, but that

had been theoretical. He'd wanted to continue the family name.

But in two months, he was going to be responsible for a real flesh-and-blood little boy. How would he know what to do? He'd assumed he'd love his child, but what if he didn't? After the way he'd been raised, how would Alex possibly know how to be a good father?

"It's nearly midnight," the elderly French lady said as she pulled away from her great-niece's embrace in the restaurant. "Are you sure you don't want to wait to leave until morning?"

Rosalie glanced back at him questioningly. Alex thought of her tiny bed in the garret, of the way it had felt with the two of them pushed together in such a tight space. He wouldn't last two minutes without trying to kiss her.

"We should leave," he replied. "We will sleep in Paris. Goodbye, *madame*." He gave Odette Lancel a small bow. "Thank you again for your assistance."

The white-haired Frenchwoman's eyes narrowed as she looked up at him. "Take good care of her, young man. Or you'll have me to deal with."

"I would not wish to tangle with you, *madame*." It was not a jest. She reminded him of his Italian grandmother, who'd been fierce and almost diabolically clever. A woman not to be crossed.

"I have your word?"

He paused. He was careful with his word. It was no longer in his soul to give flimsy promises. "Yes."

The older woman nodded, satisfied, then gave her grand-niece one last admonition. "Remember. Let him pay for everything."

"Tatie!" Rosalie seemed scandalized and her cheeks blushed deeper than ever as she threw him a nervous glance.

Ah. So that was why she'd had a change of heart about letting him pay. Her aunt had convinced her.

Alex was glad. He wanted to pay. It made things easier. And money meant little to him. Just piles of gold in the bank reminding him of things of which he did not want to be reminded. He hefted Rosalie's bag higher on his shoulder. "We should go."

She nodded. Giving her great-aunt's wrinkled cheek one last kiss, she followed him out of the restaurant. Holding her hand so she wouldn't fall, he led her down the steep hill and through the dark, deserted village.

They exited the town gate. Rosalie stopped abruptly on the flat sandy beach between the ramparts and the causeway.

"What," she breathed, "is that?"

"This?" He casually continued walking toward the red Lamborghini. He glanced back at her. "It's our ride."

"How did you get permission to park it here?" She looked at him accusingly. "There are rules."

He shrugged. "I have friends."

"I bet," she muttered as he opened the passenger door. He supported her arm as she lowered herself heavily into the black leather seat. She glared up at him. "Does everyone do what you say, wherever you go?"

"Usually," Alex said. He thought the lie sounded more modest than the actual truth, which was *Yes*.

Tucking her bag into the tiny trunk, Alex got into the driver's seat and started the engine. The low purr built to a roar as he whirled the sleek red sports car back down the empty causeway. Silence fell as he drove onto the mainland, then away across the fields of Normandy.

"Why are we driving to Venice?" she asked finally, looking uncomfortable in the supple leather seat, as if she was afraid to touch anything in the expensive car. "It would be much faster to fly."

"I don't care for planes," he said shortly, looking ahead at the empty road.

"I'm surprised you don't have a private jet."

He didn't answer. He felt her gaze on him.

"You do, don't you?" she said slowly. "You have a private jet."

"I inherited it. I allow my employees to use it. Or to bring people to me in Venice."

"Why don't you like to fly?"

Focusing fiercely on the road, he said, "My father loved it. He thought himself quite a pilot, until he crashed his Cessna into the Alps, with my mother and brother aboard."

She sucked in her breath. "Oh, no! Were they—all right?"

"No," he said flatly.

"They died?" Rosalie choked out, "I'm so sorry."

So much sympathy she had for people who hadn't been good or kind. "We were never particularly close."

"No wonder you're nervous about flying."

"I'm not nervous. I just don't do it."

She hesitated. "There are courses, classes you can take to help—"

"Yes," he cut in. "I took them. I was in the middle of one when my sister died three years ago. In a plane crash in South America." He glanced at her coldly. "I lost my entire family to plane crashes, Miss Brown. Perhaps you won't harass me if I prefer to remain on the ground."

She took a deep breath.

"I'm sorry," she said quietly. "It's awful. I know."

You don't know, he wanted to snap at her. How could she?

But her parents had died too. Maybe she did know.

Rosalie looked out the window, but before she turned her head he saw a tear streaking down her cheek.

She pitied him.

Alex wondered what Rosalie would think if she knew the whole truth. How he'd indirectly caused his family to die.

His sister, Margaret, the middle child and only daughter, had been Alex's ally growing up. She'd been the peacemaker in an angry family. Thomas, the eldest brother and heir, had all the worst qualities of their parents—a hair-trigger temper, a chip on his shoulder and a habit of screaming at the slightest insult. Alex, the youngest, had learned to keep his own resentments bottled up beneath silence and sarcasm.

As Thomas would inherit the title and the responsibility for running their family's company, Margaret had buried her head in books and research. Alex similarly had fled, to study viticulture at Cornell, and he'd dreamed of starting his own wine label in America. After graduation, he'd promised his mother he'd go home for Christmas, especially since Margaret had just started her new job as a research scientist in Antarctica. But, unwilling to face the family drama, Alex had broken his promise and stayed in New York.

And so his parents and older brother, finding the holidays unmanageable without the emotional buffer of Margaret or Alex, had decided at the last moment to go skiing in the Alps.

After their deaths, Alex had found himself unable to get on a plane, even a big commercial jet. Margaret had been sympathetic at first, but as years passed, she'd finally demanded that he get his problem *sorted out* because, as she'd said during a satellite phone call from Antarctica, "I can't help you. You can only help yourself."

"I will. I promise," he'd told her.

He'd returned to Italy, where he'd focused on the old vineyard owned by the Falconeris for generations. He knew he should take an interest in the financial institution his mother had inherited in Boston, which provided the bulk of their family's fortune. But when it was threatened with a hostile takeover, he'd wanted to sell their shares, and let it go.

"You can't," Margaret had begged him from Antarctica. "It's mother's only legacy. Promise you'll go to the shareholders' meeting in two weeks and fight it. You have to convince them not to sell!"

"I promise," Alex had told her reluctantly.

But the day before the meeting, when she'd called to make sure he'd made it to Boston, he'd been forced to admit that he was, in fact, still in Italy with no intention of getting on a plane.

Margaret had been upset. "Fine, I'll go. Even though this is a really bad time to try to leave. You should have told me from the beginning that you had no intention of going."

"I'm sorry," he tried, "I never meant to—"

"Whether you meant it or not, you lied to me. I'm disappointed in you, Alex. I'll call you when I reach Boston."

It was the last time he'd ever spoken to his sister.

Everyone said the two crashes were totally unrelated. His father had been piloting a private jet, and drinking, and likely arguing both with his wife and with his eldest son, screaming as he always did, causing them to scream back. While Margaret had been traveling to Chile on a chartered jet when a bird strike blew through the engine. There was no obvious connection between the two incidents.

Only Alex knew that there was.

Him.

If he had been honest with himself about his fear of flying, he could have booked passage on a ship to Boston in plenty of time for the shareholders' meeting. If he'd been honest with his sister, he could have told her frankly that he'd never intended to help run the investment firm. Either way, he'd broken promises, forcing his sister to leave her research station in Antarctica. Just as he'd broken that promise to his mother to come home for Christmas.

At Margaret's funeral in Venice, dry-eyed, numb, Alex came to a decision. He obviously had no idea how to love anyone. But he would never break a promise again. For any reason.

His family's investment firm had been lost in the hostile takeover, and Alex had let it go. He'd quietly accepted a fortune in cash for his family's shares. He'd tucked away the money and buried himself at the vineyard, blocking everything from his mind except the need to produce a truly stellar wine—as if that could save him.

A month later, he'd married Chiara Vulpato.

Now, as Alex drove his red Lamborghini through desolate French valleys, he looked at the beautiful woman beside him. She'd fallen asleep beneath the quietly vibrating hum of the engine. Even as she slept, her arms were cradled tenderly around her belly.

Rosalie thought she shared the same grief, because she, too, was an orphan. But her heart was full of love, and she had the naive belief that she could make the world a better place. Her parents had died in a wildfire. It hadn't been Rosalie's fault.

So she had no idea how Alex felt. At all.

And he intended to keep it that way.

Hours later, as he pulled the sports car into the grand entrance of his favorite Parisian luxury hotel, he looked at her. She'd slept fitfully for hours as they'd traveled across the north of France. She was so beautiful, so unconsciously sensual. He wanted her.

But he could not have her.

Of all women on earth, Rosalie was the most

forbidden. The stakes were too high, with a child that would bind them for the rest of their lives. She was a romantic with a loving heart. If Alex seduced her, all he would do was break that heart and wreck her life. Just as he'd wrecked so many others.

Turning off the car engine, he looked at her again, seeing the tired circles beneath her eyes as she slept. He thought of how much she had gone through over the past year. No wonder she'd been so deliriously happy when, in Venice, he'd told her she could keep her baby. No wonder she'd pulled him fiercely into her arms. He could still feel the electricity of her lips brushing against his earlobe as she'd whispered, *Thank you. You're a good man.*

But her horrified, traumatized expression when he'd shown up at her great-aunt's restaurant today told a different story. He'd made her dream of keeping her baby come true.

Then today, he'd taken it away.

He took a deep breath. He could not let her take his child away. Nor could he be the man she needed. He'd never be a romantic partner or a husband.

But there were other things he could do for her. Other ways to comfort her after all her grief. She was pregnant with his baby. She deserved every ounce of his care.

And she would get it. He thought suddenly of

her wistful words. *I just got a passport and traveled across the ocean for the first time in my life.* He remembered the Agatha Christie paperback he'd seen in her satchel.

Reaching out, Alex gently shook her awake in the stopped car beneath the illuminated porte cochere. "We're here."

"Here?"

"Paris. Our hotel."

Yawning, Rosalie blinked groggily. "What time is it?"

"Three in the morning." Looking at her sleepy expression, he smiled. "I can carry you inside, if you like."

That seemed to wake her up. She drew back, alarmed. "No. I'm awake."

As the hotel's valet rushed forward, Alex carried her bag, and his own, as he led Rosalie inside the luxurious hotel.

Even Paris was quiet at this time of night. They walked together through the elegant lobby.

He would take care of her, Alex reiterated to himself. He would give her the world.

And he would not seduce her. He could resist. Of course he could. He could resist anything.

But when they reached the registration desk, as the manager's face lit up and greeted him by name, asking if he'd like his usual room, Alex refused. He asked instead for a two-bedroom suite.

He thought of himself as tough. He'd even been

accused of being heartless. But even he could feel his weakness where Rosalie Brown was concerned.

Against her sensual beauty, he was only a man.

Rosalie woke slowly. Her eyes fluttered, then opened.

She'd slept in late. She saw it by the slant of gray light in the magnificent Paris hotel suite, all pale pastel furniture and matching silk wallpapers. She looked at the elegant clock above the marble fireplace mantel and saw it was almost noon.

She'd slept better than she'd ever imagined. But then, Alex had insisted on giving her the only bed.

Sitting up, she looked across the open suite. But on the other side of the large, spacious room, the sofa was empty.

Last night, the manager had regretfully informed them that all the two-bedroom suites were occupied. "But," he'd added hopefully, "we do have your regular room available, *monsieur le comte*. Room 847."

With a sigh, Alex had agreed. Refusing the offer of assistance with the two small satchels, he'd signed the receipt then taken her up to the hotel room himself. She'd been dazzled by the vast, bcautiful room, which seemed to her as elegant as Versailles, with its enormous bed and marble fireplace. Then she'd looked again at the bed. Just one bed.

"You will take it," Alex had told her. When Rosalie had tried to refuse, he'd asked her, with a gleam in his dark eyes, if he needed to physically lift her onto the bed himself.

The idea of having Alex hold her so closely against his body had made her afraid—afraid of herself, afraid of what she might do when faced with such temptation. So she'd agreed. Just the hours together in the tiny space of his sports car had been bad enough. She'd spent a long time pretending to be asleep, until she had actually fallen asleep.

But in the intimacy of the hotel room, after she'd already changed her clothes, brushed her teeth, climbed into the bed and pulled the blankets up to her neck, she'd heard him take off his clothes in the darkness. The slight gleam of light from the windows had caressed his naked chest as he walked to the sofa. Even though the lights were off, even though she was on the other side of the room, she still felt him. Every step. Every breath.

As she'd squeezed her eyes shut, she'd known she wouldn't sleep a wink. But she'd been more tired than she'd realized. Now, waking up so late, she felt guilty. He obviously hadn't slept nearly so well. "Alex?"

He came in from the sliding door that led to a wrought-iron balcony. "Good morning."

He looked handsome, freshly showered and shaved and wearing clean clothes, a charcoal tailored shirt and trousers. His hair was still a little wet. Unconsciously, she licked her lips. She could only imagine how she looked, with sleep-mussed hair, probably with a little drool left on her pillow. As if she didn't feel ungainly enough, at seven months' pregnant and wearing an old T-shirt that stretched over her belly like a beach balloon. "Why did you let me sleep so late?"

His dark eyes were warm as they trailed over her. "I thought you needed it."

Why? Did she look that bad? "I'm sorry."

"About what?"

"It's bad enough that I made you take the sofa—"

"You didn't make me—I insisted."

"But also, because of me, we'll get a late start on the road back to Venice. I'm sure you have more important things to do than wait for me."

"Yes," he said, "speaking of that..."

She sat up straight on the bed. "What?"

"I've decided I'm not in such a hurry." He smiled. "You said earlier that this is your first trip to Europe."

"Yes," she said, feeling suddenly guarded. "So?"

He came closer to the bed, looking down at her in a way that made her feel like the stretchy T-shirt and blanket covering her body weren't nearly enough, because she could feel him, even without him touching her.

"I've made plans."

"P-plans?" she stammered, her cheeks flooding with heat. Her gaze fell to his thighs so close to her mattress, his muscular, powerful body seeming barely tamed by his civilized clothing. "What plans?"

"Would you like to see Paris?"

Her lips parted as she looked at him. "Um?"

"I'm guessing you haven't seen much of the city."

"That's true." After she'd left him in Venice three days before, she'd gotten the cheapest flight she could to Paris. She'd stumbled out of Charles de Gaulle Airport, exhausted from jet lag, and caught the first train to Rennes, then taken the bus to arrive in a heap on her great-aunt's doorstep. She said honestly, "Last night was the most I've seen of Paris."

He snorted. "Since you were asleep, that isn't much." He paused, tilting his head as his black eyes glinted. "Get up."

Nervously, she pushed back the covers. She felt his eyes skim over her stretchy T-shirt and shorts, and her body reacted as if he'd caught her naked. She said defensively, "It's the only thing that still fits to sleep in."

"I will buy you new clothes."

She started to protest, then realized he was likely wanting to buy her new clothes just for self-preservation. For a man as sleekly sophisticated as Alex Falconeri, seeing her in an old, worn T-shirt and tiny shorts likely hurt his eyeballs. Remembering Great-aunt Odette's adjuration to *let him pay*, she sighed. "If you must."

Alex slowly looked her over again. "I must." He abruptly looked away. "But not today. Today we..."

"We what?"

"Today I'm going to show you Paris."

And Alex did. After they came out of the five-star hotel on the Champs-élysées, with Rosalie wearing just a simple blouse and flowing skirt against the cool, drizzly gray day, she discovered a Rolls-Royce and French-speaking driver, who tipped his hat.

"Mademoiselle."

She looked at Alex in surprise. "What happened to your Lamborghini?"

"I had it sent on," he said.

"Sent on? All the way to Venice?"

He shrugged, then held out his hand. "We have other things to do."

For the rest of the day, they saw the most famous sights of Paris. Traveling in luxury and comfort, they bypassed lines. Doors fell open to them as if by magic. The Eiffel Tower was first, followed by lunch at the most difficult-to-book restaurant in the City of Light. Afterward, they enjoyed a speed tour of the Louvre, including the *Mona Lisa*. Then they visited the Arc de Triomphe, the bookstores of Saint-Germain-des-Prés and ate buttery fresh-baked croissants in the Marais.

Through it all, Alex was beside her, telling her stories about the history of the city, about this shocking general, or that scandalous queen.

"How did you learn all this?" Rosalie blurted out in the back of the Rolls-Royce as twilight finally fell across the city.

"I lived here long ago, studying wine." He shook his head. "But don't ask me about that, or I will bore you to tears with stories of vintners that are not quite so interesting, unless you're fascinated by the Great French Wine Blight of 1871."

"Fascinated," she repeated, staring at the curve of his sensual lips.

"In the mid-nineteenth century, the phylloxera aphid blight destroyed most vineyards in France, forcing winemakers to try an American's crazy idea of grafting hardy Texas rootstock onto their vines. It worked, the vineyards were saved, and a cowboy was awarded the Légion d'honneur by the French government..."

She watched his lips move as he spoke, wondering what it would feel like if he kissed her.

"Rosalie." His voice was suddenly low and hoarse. "Don't."

She looked up. "What?"

"Just don't. I want to take good care of you. But there are some things I cannot do." He looked abruptly out the window. "We're almost there."

Humiliation made her cheeks blaze. Why did she keep doing this, revealing her desire? They'd spent a lovely day together, he'd been gentlemanly and kind, and she'd wrecked it all by staring at his lips!

Why did she keep embarrassing herself, forcing Alex to remind her that she could never be more to him than the mother of his child, a partner, or maybe if she was very lucky, a friend?

"Thank you for showing me Paris." She looked out at the twinkling lights of the city beneath the rising purple night. Her stomach rumbled. "Are we going to dinner?"

"Yes. But you'll have to wait for it." The car stopped outside the Gare de l'Est. "Here."

As she got out of the Rolls-Royce, she tilted her head back to look at the nineteenth-century building. "We're eating at the train station?"

"We'll be eating on the train." He grinned. "Call it fast food." Looking at her expression, Alex gave a low laugh. Taking the two satchels from the driver, he said, "Follow me."

He led her into the train station. When she finally saw their train, her jaw dropped. It was a good thing she wasn't carrying a bag, because her knees went weak.

"Our train is…is…" She swallowed hard, then breathed, "The Orient Express?"

Alex smiled almost shyly. "I saw your book, and I thought…"

Putting her arms around him, Rosalie lifted up on her tiptoes and kissed him.

It was meant to be a quick kiss, just to express her overwhelming gratitude for what he'd done for her today. His actions had gone beyond kindness. That he had noticed her paperback, and on a whim, changed their plans for returning to Venice!

Her kiss was meant to simply thank him. Nothing more. Or so she told herself.

But when their lips brushed, she felt a sizzle of electricity that shook her deep inside. She quickly pulled away, and their eyes locked on the platform of the Gare de l'Est, where they stood next to the shining carriage of their luxury train.

The two satchels fell from Alex's shoulders. Looking at her intently, he cupped her face with both his large hands and lowered his head swiftly to hers.

His kiss was not gentle. It had nothing to do with gratitude.

His lips seared hers, burning her. She gasped

as her whole world swirled around her, around the train platform in Paris, as the most handsome, powerful man she'd ever met held her tightly to his muscular body and plundered her mouth in the most amazing kiss of her life.

When he finally pulled away, Rosalie was dazed, lost. Sprinkles of stars, a penumbra of rainbow-colored fairy dust, hovered on the edges of her vision.

"What—was that?" she breathed.

"Don't you know? Haven't you guessed?" Alex looked down at her. Running his fingertips along the edge of her cheek, he said huskily, "I want you, Rosalie."

For a moment, she was lost in the dark fire of his gaze. She heard a loud whistle, and a conductor calling out in French before he said in English, with good humor, "Young lovers, do you need help with your bags?"

Blushing, Rosalie turned back to Alex.

"We're supposed to board," she said, somewhat lamely.

"Yes. I heard him." A lazy smile lifted to Alex's lips. He picked up the two satchels from the platform. "Shall we?"

She followed him, feeling like she'd fallen into an alternate universe. Alex Falconeri, the Conte di Rialto, had kissed her. He'd said he wanted her.

No. It couldn't be true. She had to be dreaming!

But as he helped her up the train steps, Rosalie

felt his hand against the curve of her lower back. And she shivered, caught between desire and fear, as they boarded the Orient Express bound for Venice.

CHAPTER FIVE

HE NEVER SHOULD have kissed her.

As the evening passed, and they'd boarded the train and found their separate compartments, Alex despised himself for his weakness. Even as he'd escorted Rosalie to their dining car and they sat across from each other for the elegant four-course meal, an underlying sexual tension had filled in all the spaces between their awkward dinner conversation, and he'd seen the unspoken question in her eyes.

What about his kiss? What did it mean? And above all: *Would it happen again?*

He would not let himself seduce her. He could not give her the love or the kind of marriage she clearly dreamed of. But he intended to make her happy. So he'd spent the whole day in Paris trying to charm her, to make her glad she'd agreed to move to Italy—while at the same time, keeping his emotional and physical distance.

Then he'd ruined it all by kissing her at the Gare de l'Est.

No matter how beautiful Rosalie had looked, no matter how wildly his body had reacted when she'd thrown her arms around him and pressed her soft lips to his, he should never have lost control and kissed her back.

After that kiss, he'd desperately needed a cold shower, and sadly his private compartment on the refurbished 1920s-era train did not have one. He deliberately hadn't booked the grand suite for two, with its anachronistic large bed and en suite shower. He was grimly determined to keep his distance.

Especially at night.

After sharing the hotel suite with Rosalie in Paris, Alex had known he could not endure another such night, tossing and turning on the sofa, aware that just a few steps away in the darkness, this beautiful, half-naked woman was wrapped around the pillows of a king-size bed. Just seeing her yesterday morning in a thin T-shirt which showed the detailed shape of her belly, her nipples and swollen breasts, and the little knit sleep shorts that rested below her pregnant tummy, clinging to the very edge of her hips as if they might fall off!

It was torture.

To be fair, in his overheated state, anything and everything felt like too much. Throughout their Paris tour yesterday, he'd been constantly aware of her, sitting beside him in the back seat of the Rolls. So he'd talked too much, tried to distract himself from his desire by telling one absurd tale after another. Even now, he could hardly believe he'd told Rosalie about the wine blight of 1871.

He'd never felt so out of control.

Alex could not seduce her. It would cause a world of hurt—not just for him, not even just for her, but for their child. Warm and sweet as she was, Rosalie would inevitably end up offering him her heart, and he would just as inevitably break it, because he had no heart of his own to offer in return. And their child would be the one to suffer most from his parents' unavoidable warring.

Alex's own parents had hated each other. For the entirety of their marriage, they'd screamed at each other, threatening divorce. His mother had cried, throwing dishes and jewels—whatever was close to hand—whenever she caught his father in another affair with a trashy stripper. His father, for his part, yelled that his affairs were her fault, because she was a drunkard, a cold harpy without a soul. They'd both started divorce proceedings multiple times, holding splashy, emotional press conferences accusing each other of cruelty and adultery, before ultimately deciding to remain together, *for the children*. The newspapers had loved the Conte and Contessa di Rialto. Already renowned for their wealth and beauty, they'd become the Italian Liz Taylor and Richard Burton, infamous for their marital battles.

But the experience had been not so enjoyable for their children.

All that drama. All that emotion. Alex had heard his parents had loved each other passionately when they wed, before all their love turned to hatred, and their vows to broken promises.

He wanted no part of that life. He'd vowed to be different. And he was. He had rules. He was honorable. For the last three years, he'd made absolutely sure to keep every single promise he made. At any cost. It was better to have no emotion at all, than risk that kind of destructive chaos.

He never should have kissed her.

And now he was paying the price. As much as he'd wanted Rosalie before, after last night's kiss on the railway platform, he could now think of nothing else but the sweet, hot fire of her lips. The desperate ache set his entire body aflame. He hungered for her like a starving man.

It had taken all Alex's strength to leave Rosalie after their dinner last evening, bidding her goodnight at the door of her compartment, with its large window and folded-down twin bed. She'd seemed shocked, even hurt, as he'd simply left her with nothing more than a courteous bow.

His sleep last night, in his lonely berth beneath the steady hum and shake of the train, had been troubled with sensual dreams. The next day, after brooding over a continental breakfast of hot coffee and orange juice and freshly baked croissants served in his compartment, Alex went to the restaurant car to meet Rosalie for lunch at noon, as they'd previously agreed.

Arriving first at the small table, Alex looked out at the magnificent view flying past the train windows as he waited for Rosalie. They'd left all the gray drizzle of Paris behind, and now he could see the green Alps and sparkling mountain lakes beneath a blue sky.

He could hear the excited, happy chatter of other Orient Express passengers, many of whom had booked this expensive trip to mark an important occasion. Half the couples around him seemed to be celebrating their wedding anniversary.

Feeling suddenly surly, Alex drank black coffee, bitter as the brew.

Looking up, he saw Rosalie in the doorway. She looked fresh and pretty, wearing a yellow sundress. Her dark hair flowed over her shoulders, and her long, tanned legs ended in open-toed sandals. People's eyes turned to her, and he rose to his feet.

Smiling shyly, she came forward and let Alex help her into her chair. The waiter came to take her drink order. *"Madame?"*

"Orange juice," she responded with a warm smile. "With ice, please."

Not just the restaurant car, but the whole world seemed suddenly brighter to Alex as he looked at Rosalie's beautiful face, listening as she exclaimed how much she loved the train, how well she'd slept last night, how breathtaking the view was outside.

Alex's coffee no longer tasted bitter as he drank in his own view of her. His gaze traced down the curve of her cheek, to the edge of her chin, to her long, graceful neck.

"It's a good thing I packed sundresses and not jeans." Rosalie turned to him with smiling eyes. "Everyone is so dressed up—"

"You could wear anything or nothing," he murmured, "and you'd still be the most beautiful woman here."

Her smile faltered as electricity crackled between them. Their table for two was an island of sparks and fire, surrounded by the happy conversations, and beneath it all, the steady hum of the train.

"I'm glad you slept well." Against his will, Alex leaned forward. "Did you dream?"

Rosalie's cheeks turned pink, and she looked up with visible relief as the waiter appeared with her glass of orange juice. She seemed afraid to meet Alex's eyes. Sipping her drink, she looked out at the sharp green mountains and vivid blue sky. Her hand seemed to tremble.

He was torturing her, Alex realized. Torturing them both. It was unfair, even cruel of him to ask about her dreams. Why had he told her she was beautiful? In this one case, honesty did not seem like the best policy. Especially since she seemed so innocent. He knew from her dossier that she was twenty-five. He wondered how many lovers she'd had. Perhaps only three? Four?

"Where are we now?" she asked him, lifting her glass to her lips. For a moment, he was distracted. Then he realized she was asking a literal question, not a metaphorical one.

"Austria, almost to the Italian border." He tried to change the subject. "I have a second cousin who lives not too far from here, in the Italian Lake District."

"A cousin!" Looking astonished, she set down her glass as the waiter served the first course of their lunch, braised artichokes *à la barigoule* served with hot, flaky rolls. "I didn't know you had any family."

"Family is relative," he said grimly. He looked at her in surprise when he heard her snort.

"You made a joke," she pointed out.

He rolled his eyes. "Hardly much of a joke."

"True, but who am I to judge?" Taking a bite, she sighed in pleasure, then tilted her head. "What's your cousin like?"

"*Second* cousin. I barely know him." That wasn't entirely true. Alex and Cesare had been friends as boys, when their parents had summered together in the Alps. But Cesare's parents being what they were, and Alex's parents being what they were, it didn't last long before the summer dissolved into bickering, shouting and drunken accusations of adultery.

But before that, for a few weeks, Cesare had been the older brother Alex had always wanted. While his real brother Thomas ignored or bullied him, his much older cousin had been gruffly kind, taking Alex fishing, skipping rocks across the lake, biking. Looking back, it had been the best summer of his life.

After that, he didn't see Cesare for years. The man had been busy building his hotel empire, and later, Alex had heard he'd gotten scandalously married to some American maid or housekeeper or something like that.

But by then, Alex's parents and older brother had died, and his sister was living in Antarctica. Alex had retreated into his own pursuit of winemaking. It was easier to think of himself as having no family than remember the one summer when he had.

Cesare had come to his family's funerals, but the two men hadn't spoken much. And Alex had invited him to his wedding, of course. The man was powerful, not to mention a prince, so Chiara had begged to include him. Why not?

At first, when he'd seen Cesare across the grand ballroom during the wedding reception, Alex had been honestly glad to see him again.

Then he'd met Cesare's wife, Emma, the lovely

dark-haired woman looking up at her husband with eyes glowing with love. He'd seen Cesare's two children, a toddler and a fat, chortling baby, both of whom clung to their father. He'd seen the way Cesare circled his family with his powerful arms, loving them back with all his heart, strength and devotion.

Then Alex had looked at his own new bride. Chiara had been drunk before she'd even spoken her vows, and avoided being near him as much as possible, including at their reception. And something had cracked inside him.

He'd spoken to Cesare and his family politely at the reception that day—but only just. And ever since, he'd avoided them. He'd evaded Cesare's attempts at organizing get-togethers, ignored Princess Emma Falconeri's chirpy Christmas cards, full of happy pictures of their growing family, and handwritten notes: "Alex, we'd love to see you!"

As if he'd ever want to visit their home at Lake Como, to see what Cesare had become. All that sloppy, ridiculous happiness. It was obscene. It wouldn't last. Any moment now, the man's marriage, his family, would all fall apart, devolving into screams and accusations and plates exploding against walls. It would. Because it always did.

Brooding, Alex stared out at the last of the Alps flying past them.

"You're not close to your cousin?" Rosalie sounded disappointed.

"Second cousin," he repeated stiffly, "and no. Not since we were boys. He's busy. He runs a large company. He has a wife. Children."

"I'd think that would make you want to see him more, not less."

"It doesn't," Alex said shortly.

She waited patiently for him to explain. He didn't.

Narrowing her eyes, Rosalie looked at him, almost as if she could see into his soul. He shifted uncomfortably in his cushioned chair. Luckily, they were interrupted by the second course.

She took a bite of lobster in butter and gasped, closing her eyes at the taste. She licked her plate before the waiter took it. Which almost made *him* gasp.

Next, the main course was served, beef in truffle sauce and fingerling potatoes. Alex noted the delicious flavor indifferently. The tantalizing pleasure he truly wanted was the woman sitting across from him at the table. The woman now moaning softly in pleasure as she ate.

A silent curse went through him. To distract her, he reintroduced the conversation. "Cesare and I have hardly seen each other since my childhood."

Rosalie blinked, slowly pulling the fork from

her mouth. It nearly made him groan aloud. "But he lives so close to Venice."

"They are often in London and Rome. He came to my sister's funeral three years ago. And my wedding a month later."

"I'm so sorry about your sister." She paused. "You were married just a month after her funeral?"

Again she waited; again, he didn't explain. He said only, "My second cousin and I lead very different lives."

She looked at him narrowly as the train hummed around them, and the dappled sunlight shone briefly on his face.

"But still," she said finally, "you're family."

"That doesn't mean anything."

"Of course it does."

Alex shrugged. "Just because someone is family doesn't mean they can't also be strangers."

Rosalie's forehead creased. "You can't be serious."

"Why?"

"Because it's messed up!" Good mood evaporated, she dropped her fork with a clatter against her empty plate. "Your cousin lives within driving distance of Venice, but you can't be bothered with him. While my great-aunt lives in France, on the other side of the world from California, but I still make an effort, phone calls, even letters! I would do anything to stay close to her. Anything!" She shook her head at the waiter, refusing the cheese plate. "She's all I have!"

She looked near tears. Reaching out, Alex gently put his hand over hers.

"That's not true. Not anymore," he said in a low voice. He looked at her belly. "We have our son."

He felt her hand tremble as she looked up at him.

"And you?" Rosalie whispered. "Will I have you?"

A shiver went through him. He pulled his hand away.

"I never should have kissed you, Rosalie," he said quietly. "It was a mistake."

"*Madame? Monsieur?* Dessert? Coffee?"

She shook her head at the waiter, as did Alex. The waiter, looking disappointed, swiftly departed.

Looking down, Rosalie twisted the linen napkin in her hands. "I wondered why you did that. Because you can't possibly—" her voice dropped so low, it was almost inaudible "—want me."

"You're wrong," he said huskily. "I want you. As I've never wanted anyone."

For a moment, their eyes locked.

Then he shook his head. "But I can never give in to it. For your sake."

She stiffened. "For—my sake?"

"Forgive me," he said softly. "But I do not

think you could give me your body without also giving me your heart. You would want a commitment. You would want a lifetime of love."

Alex realized he was holding his breath, waiting for her answer. Why? Because he hoped she would deny it? Because he hoped she would immediately inform him that he was being insufferably arrogant and she could easily, *easily*, enjoy time with him in bed with no repercussions to the future? How wonderful it would be if—

"You're right," Rosalie said. She blinked fast, trying to smile. "I think I do want forever."

It was exactly what he'd known she would say. But still, he felt unaccountably disappointed.

"I have no desire for a one-night stand," she continued. "It would feel empty. I want…more."

"You want love," he agreed.

She looked up. "I want a marriage like my parents had. I know that probably sounds silly. But that's why I've waited."

"What do you mean—waited?" He rolled his eyes, shaking his head. "It's not like you're some untouched virgin…"

She looked studiously at the white linen tablecloth. "Yes."

He frowned, confused. "Yes what?"

"I'm—" Blushing, she ducked her head as she whispered, "What you said. I've never…" She looked away, her eyes affixed on a random chalet on the other side of the mountain valley.

The world dropped from under his feet.

"You cannot mean," he croaked, "you've never had sex?"

Glancing sharply to the right and left, as if she feared one of the long-married couples nearby might have heard his words, she shook her head.

"But you can't be a virgin," he stammered, still unable to comprehend it. "You're *pregnant*."

"Yes." He must have looked comical, because looking at him, she gave a rueful laugh. "I wondered a little, that no one at the fertility clinic stopped me from being a surrogate. I gather it's usually a problem. But your—Chiara must have paid them to look the other way." She said wistfully, "I wanted to wait for true love. To be intimate with only one person. For a lifetime." She looked up at him with a crooked smile. "Silly, huh?"

Alex's heart was pounding, his body burning. Rosalie was pregnant with his child. And yet no man had ever touched her. Not even him. She was a virgin.

He looked at her downcast eyes. She was afraid he would laugh at her. Scorn her. "Rosalie. Look at me."

Nervously, she lifted her gaze. He saw her self-consciousness. She thought he would insult her as—what? As a freak? A throwback to the Victorian age? Her eyes gleamed with fear of being hurt.

"You're right," she said suddenly. "It's stupid." She started to turn away, to rise from the table—

He grabbed her arm, knowing he couldn't let her go like this. "I honor your choice," he said quietly. "I respect it."

Her shoulders relaxed a little as she stayed in her chair. She looked at him over the table. "You do?"

Alex gave a nod. "You think of sex as part of marriage. As something to be shared with only one person."

"Yes."

"I honor sex in marriage, as well. It's part of the vows. 'To keep only unto her as long as you both shall live.' It's why I wouldn't divorce Chiara. It's why—" he lifted his eyes to hers "—even though she cheated on me for years, and we quit sharing a bed shortly after we were wed, I never betrayed those vows."

Her lips parted. "But—that would mean you've been celibate for…"

"Almost three years." Alex held his breath. Knowing well how his friends would react, he'd never shared that fact with anyone.

Rosalie stared at him with something like horror. For a moment, she closed her eyes, as if she'd just received some heavy blow. Then she slowly opened them.

"Finally," she whispered. "I understand."

* * *

And Rosalie did understand.

Ever since they'd left Mont-Saint-Michel, she'd fought her desire for him as a matter of course. Any woman would want a powerful, gorgeous, ridiculously sexy man like Alex Falconeri. But it wouldn't make any sense for *him* to want her.

And yet, innocent as she was, she'd noticed the way his gaze had lingered on her. And then, on the platform at the train station in Paris, the way he'd kissed her!

His embrace had been a wonder, magical. As he'd kissed her, all the world had whirled around them like a storm, lightning crackling through her veins. When he'd finally pulled away, she'd been lost, knowing that if they shared a compartment on the train, she could no longer resist his seduction any more than she could resist breathing.

But Alex hadn't tried to seduce her. He'd kept his distance, leaving her to read her book and sleep alone, nervously looking out at the gorgeous Alpine scenery, wondering when he'd appear, when he'd explain. After an early breakfast, she'd walked the length of the train and said hello to other smiling passengers, all of whom seemed happy to be here, as if this trip was the fulfillment of a lifelong dream. And no wonder. She could only imagine how much it cost.

But Alex had arranged it on a whim. Because

he'd noticed the old Agatha Christie paperback in her satchel.

He pretended to be cold and ruthless, but on the inside, she saw the streak of kindness that he tried to hide. He wanted to take care of her, because she was carrying his baby.

But he didn't actually desire her, Rosalie Brown of Brown Farm in Emmetsville, California. Now she finally understood.

He'd kissed her because he was *starving.*

A man like Alex Falconeri, with that level of sensual appeal, should have been well-fed sexually. But he hadn't had sex in years. No wonder he was looking at her like a starving man might look at a buffet table.

"What do you mean, *you understand*?" Alex demanded now.

"It's not me you want," she whispered, glancing around the restaurant car of the train, which luckily had started to thin out from the lunchtime crowds. "You're just starved for sex. That's the only reason you kissed me. *Any* woman would be desirable to you right now. I was just handy."

He pulled away, his dark eyes serious. "Do you truly believe that?"

Rosalie thought again of the way he'd dropped the bags on the platform and taken her in his arms with such passion when he'd kissed her, such yearning and need.

But which made more sense—that Alex, a gorgeous, aristocratic Italian billionaire, would actually desire an ordinary girl like Rosalie? Or that she was simply nearby, and he was taking what was easily available, like a starving man would grab a handy bag of chips?

She looked away. "I'm not your type."

"What's my type?"

"Blonde," she said. "Thin and beautiful and regal."

"You just described Chiara," Alex said flatly. "And I never wanted her. Not even on our wedding day. Kissing her was like kissing a flagpole in winter."

Rosalie caught her breath. He really felt that way about someone so stylish, so effortlessly beautiful? "Then why did you marry her?"

"We both came from a similar background. I thought a marriage would work." He paused. "And her family's winery was next to mine."

"You make it sound so cold-blooded. Like a business merger."

"That's what it was. There was very little desire in it, for either of us. She was in love with another man."

"Why did she marry you, then?"

"Because her father had threatened to disinherit her if she threw her life away on some penniless musician. And if there was one thing that Chiara valued even more than her lover, it was having money."

"And that's what you think marriage is?" Rosalie recoiled. "You all sound so awful."

"Yes," he said.

She suddenly hated that her unborn baby had anything to do with any of them. "If I'd known—"

"If you'd known," Alex agreed.

For a moment, Rosalie felt a bittersweet lump in her throat. "I wish I'd conceived this baby the old-fashioned way," she said wistfully, looking at her belly. "I wish I'd waited for a husband I could trust and believe in."

"You can believe in me," Alex said. She looked up. "I promise you, Rosalie. I will always be there for our son. I will be the best father I can."

She exhaled. She knew what such a promise meant to him.

"Thank you for that, at least." She hesitated. "And if I someday find a man I want to marry?"

His dark eyes widened, then he gave a small smile. "All I ask is that he is worthy of my son. And of you."

Rosalie was still thinking of those words much later that afternoon, when the Orient Express finally crossed the causeway into Venice.

The sun was setting, leaving the sky aflame with red and orange that reflected back from the lagoon, and the Grand Canal outside Santa Lucia station as they arrived.

Alex helped her down the steps from the train,

lifting their satchels against his powerful shoulder. "My driver is waiting outside."

Rosalie looked at his powerful frame in the expensively cut shirt and trousers. The hard lines of his jaw, dark with five o'clock shadow, his sculpted cheekbones, his black eyes that seemed at times as fathomless as night, containing all the mysteries of the universe. They all made up Alex. The greatest mystery of all.

He hadn't wanted Chiara, as beautiful as she'd been. Was it actually possible…somehow…that he wanted Rosalie? Not just because she was handy, but because…

Because why? Why on earth would he want her?

She pondered the question silently as his driver, at the helm of a luxurious speedboat rather than a car, drove them through the canals back to Alex's palazzo.

Why would a sexy billionaire like the Conte di Rialto want her, when no ordinary man ever had?

Although that wasn't entirely true, she realized. A few boys in her rural high school had competed for her attention. Then there was Cody from the farm next door, whose awkwardly sweet proposal had set her parents' hearts racing—and Rosalie fleeing to San Francisco. During her time in the big city, she'd been far too busy and too overwhelmed to be thinking of dating anyone, especially as she'd watched her roommates engage in one empty hookup after another. But Rosalie had to admit she *had* been asked out by customers and coworkers. Only she'd thought of those attempts as something to be evaded. The last thing she'd wanted to do was hurt anyone's feelings. So she'd kept her head down, avoiding any man's attention.

As the speedboat pulled up to the private dock behind the palazzo, Rosalie glanced at Alex from beneath her dark lashes. Could he actually want her? Was it possible?

Then as he helped her out, and they walked through the private gate into the luxurious, formal rooms of the palazzo, she abruptly decided it didn't matter.

Because as he'd said, their kiss had been a mistake. He didn't intend to marry again, and *she* wasn't interested in a one-night stand. Their baby deserved a stable home, a stable family.

Even if Rosalie did not. Not really. Not after the way she'd abandoned her parents to their fate. A lump rose to her throat.

Alex turned to her at the bottom of the sweeping staircase, beneath the chandelier and painted frescoes. "I'll show you to your room."

He led her upstairs to a long hallway, and then pushed open one of the doors. Inside, she saw an enormous four-poster bed, and a flower-strewn balcony that overlooked the canal.

"Will this do?" he asked quietly.

She looked from the antique writing desk, to

the elegant chair beside it, to the shelves filled with leather-bound books. A portrait of some supercilious Circe in seventeenth-century clothes stared down from the marble fireplace. "Who is that?"

He shrugged. "Some ancestor. Or perhaps a painting bought by one for its intrinsic value. I can't keep track of them all." He opened the enormous, empty closet. "For your clothes."

As he set down her small satchel, she stared at him incredulously. "I don't need all this."

Alex smiled. "You will. I'm taking you shopping tomorrow. Right after you get a checkup with the doctor." He held up his hand to stop her protests. "I'm sorry, Rosalie, you cannot survive in Venice with just a few sundresses and a single pair of sandals. Dinner will be in one hour in the dining room. I'll leave you to freshen up. My room is next door if you need me." He paused at the door. "Thank you for coming here."

His intense gaze made her heart race faster. "You didn't leave me much choice," she said, and despised the tremble in her voice. He shook his head.

"There is always a choice." And he closed the door behind him.

Always a choice.

As Rosalie went into her en suite bathroom and took a long, hot shower, she thought about his words. Brushing out her wet hair, she took her last sundress out of the satchel, grateful it had been washed and pressed by the hotel staff in Paris. She would wear it for dinner tonight, then perhaps tomorrow, as well.

Perhaps Alex was right. At least for the foreseeable future, her life had changed. It was time to accept that. She didn't just need new clothes. She needed to call her boss and roommates in San Francisco and let them know she wouldn't be coming back.

But how long would this last? Once her stay here was finished, where would she go to start over, yet again? How would it even work for her and Alex to share custody after the baby was born?

So many questions, so few answers. With a sigh, Rosalie glanced at herself in the mirror then went downstairs to find the dining room. She stopped on the staircase when she heard voices from the foyer below.

She saw Alex speaking to a beautiful blonde woman in a tight, sexy dress. The woman was moving toward Alex with a low, intimate laugh, pressing her hand against his chest, as she said something in Italian.

Rosalie must have made a noise, for they both turned to her.

She blushed. A moment before, she'd been feeling almost pretty in the white cotton sundress, but now, compared to the other woman, she felt hugely pregnant and ungainly as a whale.

Stop it, she told herself angrily. She wasn't Alex's wife or girlfriend. Who cared if the blonde was looking at Alex like a Persian cat looked at a bowl of fresh cream? It didn't matter to Rosalie. She had no claim on his romantic life.

Forcing her lips into a warm smile, she came forward.

"Hello." She held out her hand. "I'm Rosalie."

The blonde just stared at her as if she had two heads. Her eyes dropped to Rosalie's pregnant belly, then she turned to ask Alex a sharp question in Italian.

He responded coolly in the same language.

"Fine," the woman snapped in English. "Who is this?"

"I'm Rosalie," she repeated, dropping her hand. "Rosalie Brown. Are you one of Alex's friends?"

"One of Chiara's friends," the woman said, looking at her as if she were some dog poo she'd just discovered beneath her sleek designer high heel.

"Rosalie and I just arrived home," Alex said smoothly. "So as you can see, we're busy now, Giulia. Perhaps you can visit some other time—"

"Yes, I can see how busy you've been." The blonde's heavily made-up eyes focused with laser-like focus on Rosalie's baby bump. With a sweet smile, she asked him, "The baby is yours?"

"Of course he is," Rosalie said indignantly.

Giulia gave Alex a pointed smile. "Ah, you're a sly one. All this time, everyone criticized Chiara, and thought you were so noble and long-suffering, but you didn't mind her affair at all, did you?" She looked at Rosalie's belly. "All that time you were buried in the country, you weren't just squeezing grapes."

Rosalie's jaw dropped. She'd never once imagined that anyone could think that she and Alex had conceived the baby the old-fashioned way—that they'd had some kind of adulterous affair while he was still married!

"You've got it wrong," she said indignantly. "Alex and I only met last week. I'm a surrogate. This baby was conceived in a fertility clinic in California. Chiara hired me."

"She hired you?" The other woman was incredulous. "Are you telling me that Chiara is the actual mother of your baby? That you're only the oven, as it were?"

"No," Rosalie was forced to admit. "The bun—I mean the baby—is mine, but it was Chiara's idea—"

The woman gave a low laugh. "It's the most ridiculous story I've ever heard. How delicious." Looking up at Alex, she purred, "You will still come tomorrow, won't you? You won't be too *busy* to attend an event in honor of your dead wife?" She glanced at Rosalie's belly, then gave a wicked smile. "If you don't show up, people will think you're hiding something."

"I have nothing to be ashamed of," he said coldly.

"Good. Oh, and bring her, won't you?" Giulia waved her red-tipped hand toward Rosalie. "Everyone will be dying to meet her."

Going to the door, he opened it. "Ciao, Giulia."

"Ciao."

After he closed the door, Rosalie ventured, "What was that?"

Alex gave a grim smile. "*That* was Giulia Zanella. Chiara's best friend." He rolled his eyes. "Though that didn't stop her from throwing herself at me multiple times throughout my marriage. Even on the night of Chiara's funeral."

"*What?* What kind of horrible friend—?"

"She is holding a charity ball tomorrow night in honor of her *dear dead friend*, to raise money for a local musicians' fund. Really just in honor of herself, if you ask me..."

"So why would you go?" she cried.

"If I don't, they'll say I was afraid. That I was ashamed." He glanced at Rosalie's belly ruefully. "Especially now."

"Why wouldn't she believe me about the surrogacy?" she said, frustrated.

He shrugged. "Because it's more amusing for her not to believe it." He gave her an unwilling smile. "Besides. Even you have to admit the truth is hard to believe. It seems far more likely that I seduced you, than that Chiara created a baby I didn't know about on the other side of the world."

"Seriously? There's no way it's more likely you'd seduce me."

"What do you mean?"

"Well, look at you." Rosalie motioned vaguely toward his Greek-godlike beauty and sleek suit. Then she looked down at herself, with her still-wet hair leaving damp marks on the cotton bodice of her white sundress. She mumbled, "And look at me."

For a moment, silence fell in the foyer.

"I am looking at you, Rosalie," he said softly.

Electricity filled the air as she glanced up. Their eyes met. He came closer.

Suddenly, her mouth went dry. She licked her lips. Saw his gaze fall to the motion of her tongue.

"Why won't you believe you're beautiful?" He brushed back some tendrils of hair from her face. "All the more beautiful because you're not even trying to be. You just are."

Her lips parted and her heart was pounding as she looked at his sensual mouth. He was going to kiss her again. She knew it…

His hands tightened on her upper arms, then he dropped back. "I'm sorry Giulia was rude. I will not, of course, bring you with me to her charity ball to be gawked at and gossiped about." His black gaze was ferocious. "I would never wish you to endure such a thing. Come. Dinner is waiting."

But as Alex led her into the dining room, Rosalie was forced to admit what her senses had been screaming at her for days. She didn't know why, or how. But for whatever reason, it was true.

Alex wanted her.

In the elegant, oversize dining room with its chandeliers over its table for twelve, Alex pulled out a chair for her, his eyes hungry. As she came forward, no matter how she tried to tell herself that their desire didn't matter, that it was forbidden, all she could hear was the husky echo of his words.

There is always a choice.

CHAPTER SIX

FIRST THING THE next morning, as threatened, Alex took Rosalie to the best obstetrician in Venice, who'd opened up her private clinic two hours early for them.

When he first heard his baby's heartbeat and saw the sonogram, he was overcome in a way he'd never expected. He actually felt tears in his eyes. He blinked them away before either Rosalie or the doctor could notice. But as she was stretched out on the examination table, looking at the ultrasound pictures of their son, Alex reached for Rosalie's hand and held it very tight.

But other than that, he was careful not to touch her. It was too dangerous, tempting him to do more. Instead, after she'd gotten a clean bill of health from the obstetrician, who'd told them the baby would arrive in early August, Alex introduced her to her new city. They explored Saint Mark's Square early in the morning, before the cruise ships arrived. He watched her laugh as she saw the pigeons flying up against the sky.

After breakfast, they went to luxury clothing boutiques, at his insistence, and he bought her and the baby anything he wanted, anything Rosalie's gaze lingered on, even for a moment. When she protested, Alex reminded her of his promise to her great-aunt that he'd take care of them. "I do not intend to cross her."

"Probably wise," Rosalie sighed, but she seemed to find shopping uninspiring, even when he insisted on buying her a formal ball gown "just in case."

"I just don't see the point," she argued. "I don't know how long I'll be staying in Venice. It's not like I'll need any ball gowns after I leave. I doubt I'll even need one here."

Alex didn't like to think of her leaving. "I'm buying it."

"It's not necessary—"

"Pick out some dresses. Or I'll pick them for you. Then I'll drag you to the jewelry boutique and force you to pick out diamonds to match."

Faced with such an awful threat, Rosalie dutifully picked out a fancy ball gown, as well as a cocktail dress, both of which were bagged up by the delighted shopgirls. "I chose the most expensive dresses in the store," she grumbled. "I hope you're happy."

"Very," he said, but as they passed a lingerie shop, he thought he would have been even happier to buy her everything in that particular store.

He resisted. After a few more shops, as his bodyguard discreetly arranged for all the packages to be sent home, Alex turned to her with a smile. "All right. I suppose you've suffered enough. Shall we explore?"

As they explored the tiny alleys and winding byways, he entertained her with the history of the city, which had been a republic for a thousand years—even in the Middle Ages, when all the countries around them had been feudal kingdoms.

She asked him questions about what a doge was—apparently the elected leader of the council. She wanted to know when Venice had become a republic—697—and how it had ended—Napoleon.

"This city has always been fought over, by men who lusted after it to the death. It's ironic that Venice is called La Serenissima when men have gone mad trying to take it. Men have gone mad," he said in a low voice, looking at Rosalie, "trying to possess what they cannot have."

Her eyes became dreamy. "I think it's beautiful."

"Yes." The city *was* beautiful, Alex thought. But growing up here, it had always felt cold. Beautiful and cold. Like his family's palazzo. Like Chiara.

Rosalie was not cold. She was warm, like the earth. Being around her made him feel like himself, the man he really was beneath the title and vast fortune and expensive designer suits. Just as he felt most himself while overseeing the vineyards of his country estate, ninety minutes outside the city.

Venice, as beautiful as it was, had never truly felt like his home. For many reasons.

It was when they stopped for a late lunch at the most exclusive restaurant in the city that Rosalie first noticed they were being followed. As they went inside, she glanced nervously behind them at the people who were stopped by the man at the door.

"Are they following us?" she whispered.

"Yes," Alex answered grimly, as they were led to his preferred table, private in the back.

But even here, inside this elegant *ristorante*, some of their fellow diners were surreptitiously watching them. One young woman at a nearby table lifted up her phone to take a photo.

"Why are they looking at us?" Rosalie asked uncomfortably.

Alex shrugged. "People have been following us ever since we left the doctor's office. It is normal."

"Normal?" Her lovely face was shocked.

But as he enjoyed the house specialty, *spaghetti alla carbonara*, Alex looked again at the crowd outside the window, on the edge of the square. The number of people had grown exponentially since they'd arrived. *This* size of crowd was not so normal.

Suddenly, his bodyguard crossed the restaurant, whispering urgently in his ear. Tossing money on the table, Alex rose to his feet.

"I'm not done yet," Rosalie protested, holding up a fork thick with *linguine alle vongole.*

"We must go."

"Why? What's wrong?" she asked, bewildered as the bodyguard led them out the back exit.

"Someone posted a photo of us on social media," he said grimly. "And it's already gotten picked up on television and online. There's interest."

"In what?"

"In you. In us. In our apparent juicy affair during my marriage that led to your pregnancy."

She looked back at their half-eaten lunch. "But—it's not fair!"

Alex snorted incredulously. "Fair?"

He spoke the word mockingly, as if expecting fairness in the world was a fantasy believed only by children and fools. Her cheeks went red.

In the alley behind the restaurant, another waiting bodyguard whisked them into the docked speedboat. His driver Lorenzo sped them away down the canals, turning quickly from one to another. Once they were out of the sun, away from prying eyes in the cool shadows of the deep, they reached the palazzo's private gate. Behind them, in the distance, boats were desperately trying to catch up with them, but they would be too late.

Alex helped her climb out of the speedboat, where Collins was waiting inside the open gateway. He locked it behind them.

Once they were in the quiet privacy of the courtyard, Rosalie exhaled with relief. "I can't believe you deal with that all the time."

He glanced back at her as they entered the grand hallway of the palazzo. "I don't. It's why I spend most of my time in the countryside."

"You? In the country?" Her expression was doubtful. He smiled.

"I'm a farmer. I grow grapes. I make wine."

"But—aren't you this billionaire aristocrat?"

He snorted. "Have you ever heard the joke about the best way to make a small fortune in winemaking? You start with a large fortune." Tilting his head, he sighed. "Luckily I don't need to make a living." He didn't like to remember how he'd gotten the huge fortune now sitting in worldwide investments—by losing control of his mother's company. And losing his sister. His throat grew tight. "I don't chase money. That's what I like about farming. The sun and rain and earth don't give a damn about my title. They're *real*."

She looked up at the frescoes, at the grand chandelier. "But—you live in this palazzo..."

Alex motioned toward the gilded salon. "Chiara lived here. She liked the grandeur, and being close to her boyfriend and the Venice music scene. But I haven't really lived here since I was a boy. The only reason I'm here now is to tie things up."

"What things? You mean me?" Rosalie's voice quivered a little.

"I mean all the things that need to be done after someone is dead," he said flatly. "Chiara didn't leave a will. All her remaining fortune was left to me as her husband. She must be turning in her grave. And there were other legal complications to be dealt with." He paused. "Her lover left behind a wife and children."

"Wait—the man was *married*?"

He shrugged. "That's why Chiara didn't just want a divorce—she wanted my fortune to go with it. Carraro hinted that nothing less could induce him to leave his wife. My guess is he enjoyed having them both. He seemed to have no morals, but then—" he gave a grim smile "—I think that's what Chiara liked about him."

Rosalie's eyes were huge with shock. Her mouth was open, as if she could not find any words.

"I have a few things to finish sorting out with the lawyer over the next few weeks. I'll attend Giulia's charity ball, so no one can say I did not pay my respects to Chiara's memory. But after that, I'm going home." He looked at her, then added gently, "But if the city feels like home to you, we can stay."

"Home." Rosalie's voice was unexpectedly bitter. "Venice is beautiful, but it's not my home." She looked away. "I called my boss in San Francisco from the train. Told him he'll need to find a new receptionist. I left a message for my roommates too. My rent is paid till the end of the month, but I'll need to go get my stuff."

"My people can arrange it. Just give me the address."

"Thank you." She sighed. "I just wish I knew where I'll be living in the future."

"Here with me," he said, thinking it should be obvious.

Rosalie gave a rueful laugh. "Yes, but after the baby is born…"

"Here with me," he repeated firmly.

"For a while, yes," she agreed, then said in a small voice, "Then I want to find my place in the world. My permanent home."

Permanent home.

Alex wanted to tell her that her permanent home should be with him. Then he'd never need to grudgingly allow some other man into his child's life. Into Rosalie's bed.

But how could he even consider saying that, when he knew she wanted more than he could give?

How could he say it, with the memory of three miserable years of marriage still ringing in his brain?

"Was it hard to quit your job and tell your roommates goodbye?" he asked.

"No. I never felt really at home in San Francisco, either."

"Where is your home, then?"

She gave a low laugh. "Emmetsville, I guess." Her expression grew sad. "But our farm is gone. Burned. I saw it, when I went to my parents' funeral..." She shuddered. "I can never go back."

"Why not?"

She turned away, her face half-hidden by shadow. For a moment he thought she wouldn't answer. Then she said, in a voice almost too quiet to hear, "Because it's my fault. My fault my parents died."

"How can that be true? It was a wildfire, caused by lightning. Do you control the skies?"

Turning away, she started up the stairs. "I'm tired. I'm going to rest. I'll see you for dinner later."

Alex thought of pressing her, of persuading her to see that her parents' deaths obviously weren't her fault. But how could he? He himself had many things he never, ever wanted to discuss with anyone. And unlike Rosalie, the things he felt guilty about were actually his fault, and if he let himself remember, anguish would snap its bloodthirsty jaws right through his heart—

"I will be gone tonight," he said.

She stopped on the stair. "The charity ball."

He gave a single nod. "You'll be on your own. Maria can prepare any dish you like. She is a very good cook. Collins will serve it wherever you prefer, in the dining room or more casually in the breakfast room."

She shuddered a little. "And you'll have to face that awful woman, and her friends…" Biting her lip, she looked at him. "Are you sure you don't want me to come with you?"

Alex gave a rueful laugh. "*Cara*, the night is unlikely to be an enjoyable one. The last thing I'd wish to do is inflict it on you. No. Stay here, and have a peaceful evening. That will give me some solace, at least. I will see you in the morning."

"All right." She looked uncertain. "Will you come to my room to say goodbye before you leave?"

"Of course."

"Are you worried?"

He gave a small smile. "Not at all."

The truth was that Alex thought of the upcoming event with utter dread. There was sure to be a scene. But he'd be damned if he'd stay home, and let them have the satisfaction of thinking he was afraid.

After an afternoon spent on the phone with lawyers, then the manager of his vineyard, Alex reluctantly went upstairs to get ready for the ball. He paused at Rosalie's closed bedroom door, but hearing nothing, he went into his own room and took a shower.

Once dressed in his tuxedo, he again paused at her door, and this time thought he heard some movement. He lifted his hand to knock, then lowered it again. He paced back and forth in the hallway, then finally, hands clenched at his sides, he went downstairs.

In his study, he poured himself a drink, gulped it down and paced some more.

His desire for her was almost unbearable. The last thing he wanted to do was enter her bedroom.

How would he manage to live in the same house as her; how could he see her every day? How would he raise his child with her, knowing he could never touch her, knowing she could never be his?

Because Rosalie Brown wanted love, which he could never give her. He had no heart to share. If he had the capacity, wouldn't it have revealed itself by now?

He paced another three steps, his whole body tense. But how could he endure his desire for her without satiating it? How?

His friends would tell him to take a lover, he thought suddenly. Yes. A lover. A very good idea. That would be the obvious medicine for this disease. He knew dozens of women he could easily invite to his bed, if he wished. Women he could seduce with little effort.

Unfortunately, he didn't want any of them.

Exhaling, Alex stopped, clawing back his hair.

He only wanted Rosalie. But he couldn't have her. Not without destroying what chance they might have at a peaceful partnership, raising their child together.

I want to find my place in the world. My permanent home.

He had to put it from his mind. He would take care of her for the next two months until the baby was born. And then he'd take care of both her and his newborn son.

But sometime after that, he would have to let Rosalie go.

He'd always be their baby's father. But he could never be Rosalie's man. He'd have no choice but to allow her to find a husband who could love her, and love their child.

Alex's hand tightened on the glass.

He wished love had never been invented. He desired Rosalie, but more than that—he liked her. They were having a child together. They could have gotten on well together as partners. As lovers. Perhaps even as spouses.

How much better would it be for their child to be raised in a secure home, with married parents who were stable, reasonable friends, who'd never been in love so could never be in hate? Who would never scream or threaten divorce?

If Rosalie weren't so fixated on love—

The grandfather clock in his study gave a ponderous chime. It was time to leave. He set down his empty glass.

"Alex."

Hearing Rosalie's voice, he went out to the foyer.

She stood on the sweeping staircase, illuminated by the twilight, warm rose and gold, from the large window behind her. Her long dark hair tumbled down her bare shoulders. The pink satin cocktail dress showed off the curves of her pregnant body, showcasing her overflowing breasts. Her tanned legs led down to high-heeled sandals.

He was transfixed by her beauty. To his hungry gaze, she looked like a pregnant goddess, symbolizing everything sexual and feminine.

Men have gone mad trying to possess what they cannot have.

As she came down the stairs, he couldn't take his eyes off her. All he wanted to do was take her in his arms. To lift her up against his chest and carry her straight back up the stairs.

"Why are you dressed like this?" he said.

Rosalie smiled, her brown eyes glowing beneath her dramatic sweep of dark lashes.

"I couldn't let you face them alone," she said simply.

He stared at her, overwhelmed. She felt protective—of him?

The noble thing would be to refuse, to tell her

to stay here. But that seemed a churlish response to such a gesture.

Besides, Alex was forced to admit, he wanted her near him. Even though her sensual beauty tortured him, just seeing her, having her next to him, somehow made his world a better place. Selfish or not—he could not refuse her.

With a deep breath, Alex held out his arm. "So," he said with forced cheerfulness, "into the fiery pit?"

Rosalie took his arm, putting her hand lightly over the sleeve of his tuxedo jacket. She gave an awkward laugh. "There will be dessert, right? And music?"

"Yes," he said a little grimly. "There will be music."

He looked down at her fingers resting on his arm. Even that slight touch made him tremble. Three years, he thought. Nearly three years without a woman. And he wanted *this* woman more than he'd wanted any other.

Rosalie wanted him too. He could see that by the way she looked at him, the smile sliding from her face as her fingers tightened around his arm. It would be so easy to seduce her. He could take her right back upstairs and—

No. No, damn it. He could not. Would not. She wanted love. She wanted marriage. It would be dishonorable of Alex to lure her into accepting less.

He could not do love, he thought suddenly. But marriage?

Marriage…

Outside in the palazzo's courtyard, the warm twilight enfolded them. They went through the back gate, where Lorenzo waited with the speedboat. Alex gently helped her into the vehicle. As his driver accelerated the engine, the gleaming boat moved forward, slicing through pink-and-violet waves. The wind blew against Rosalie, whipping her dark hair against Alex's cheek.

This was unwise, he thought. He expected Chiara's friends to be brutal, even cruel. He never should have let Rosalie come with him tonight. He should tell Lorenzo to turn around and take her back to the palazzo, where it was safe.

But in the Venice sunset, as Rosalie turned to face him with eyes like stars, something cracked in his soul. And he could not let her go.

Alex wanted her to be his. Tonight and forever. He didn't just want her in his bed. He wanted to live with her. As his partner. As his friend. He wanted to raise their child together, in a stable, permanent home. She'd had loving parents. She could show him how to give their son a happy childhood.

He wanted Rosalie to be his wife, he realized. And to hell with the consequences.

As Rosalie stepped onto the dock near the grand palazzo where the charity ball would be held, she had a hard time taking a full breath. It had to be due to her formfitting pink cocktail dress, she told herself. She wasn't nervous. She wasn't. Her high-heeled shoes tottered as Alex led her toward the red carpet and paparazzi waiting in front of the palace's grand entrance.

But Rosalie knew she was lying to herself. She was afraid.

Because Giulia Zanella had seemed so spiteful and mean when they'd met yesterday. The woman had already spread gossip far and wide. Rosalie had heard Alex's bodyguard telling him it had been Giulia's posts on social media that had snowballed, brought crowds outside their restaurant and forced them to flee out the back door. Rosalie could only imagine how bad tonight would be, being surrounded by people who'd loved Alex's dead wife, and come together to honor her. Would all of them believe Alex had been unfaithful, and Rosalie was some kind of trashy mistress-slash-home wrecker?

And her a virgin!

It was so unfair. But remembering how Alex had mocked her for that admittedly childish complaint earlier, she didn't say that aloud.

"Are you ready for this?" Alex asked quietly, tucking her hand around his arm as they faced the crowds outside the door. With a deep breath, she nodded. Because as nervous as she was, she was totally sure about one thing: she couldn't let him face this alone.

As they walked by the paparazzi, she ignored the shouted questions and Italian words that sounded vaguely like insults, and kept her head held high. She exhaled with relief as they entered the building. But she relaxed too soon. As he led her into the grand ballroom, she quickly discovered it was a case of out of the frying pan, into the fire.

Crowds of party guests, mostly young and dressed creatively, in wild, bright colors, or else scantily, barely covering themselves, all turned to stare, some with hostility, others merely curious. A few men in tuxedoes, clearly Alex's friends, came and spoke with him quietly. They spoke in Italian, obviously astonished he'd come to enemy territory. They looked at Rosalie with something like pity.

"You made it!" Giulia was suddenly in front of them with a sharp, gleeful smile. With her extremely thin frame and tiny tight black-and-white dress, she made Rosalie think of Cruella de Vil.

"Hello," she replied politely. "Thank you for inviting me."

"Darling, you're the star attraction. Come." The blonde took Alex's other arm. "Let me show you to your table."

As they passed through the crowds, Rosalie watched as people came forward, speaking tauntingly to him in Italian. They didn't even look at Rosalie's face, only her belly. Her hands clenched. It was all she could do not to yell or run away.

A red flush crept up Alex's neck. But he did not rise to the bait. He responded to each person coolly, even coldly.

Giulia gave each interlocutor plenty of time to corner them before she moved on through the ballroom at a glacial pace.

"And here is your table," the blonde chirped finally. "Just for you lovebirds, to have some private time!"

It was a table for two, set directly beneath the podium on the stage. They were surrounded by ten-person tables.

Without comment, Alex pulled out a chair at the tiny table. As Rosalie sat in it, Giulia added with a vengeful smile, "After dinner, Alex, you'll come up on stage and say a few words about Chiara—won't you?"

If she thought she could rattle him, she was disappointed. "Of course," he replied calmly. "Whatever is needed for—what is your organization again?"

"The Venice Association for the Promotion of the Musical Arts," she said sweetly. "Chiara was a beloved benefactress."

His handsome face held no expression. "Right."

Alex sat down with Rosalie. Feeling the eyes of the other guests in the ballroom from all the larger surrounding tables, she whispered indignantly, "I'm just surprised they haven't put a spotlight on our table, to help people know where to throw their tomatoes!"

He gave a low snort, then put his hand gently over hers. "Are you all right?"

"Yes," she sighed. "And in a way, I'm glad we have our own table. But it's just so unfair! They're acting like you did something wrong when you didn't!"

"There's no point in fighting. We could show them a report from the fertility clinic and it wouldn't change their minds. People will believe what they want to believe. And besides—" he looked at her quietly "—who told you life was fair, Rosalie?"

She looked away, suddenly in tears. "My parents," she said. "They told me if you always do the right thing, try to help and be kind, that people would be kind in return."

Alex gave a low laugh. "I had a very different education in my childhood."

"What was it?"

"Kill or be killed."

She gaped at him. "You don't mean that."

As dinner was served by a bored-looking waiter, Alex looked at her with a brief smile that didn't meet his eyes. "No. Of course I don't." He looked down at the plate of food, which seemed like a very weak, pasty meal of overboiled green beans and bland chicken. "And after this, I will make a speech extolling Chiara's virtues."

"Was she really such a benefactress to music?" she asked, looking at the bohemian crowd around them.

"She was to one musician," he said wryly, before taking a sip of red wine.

With a gulp, Rosalie looked up at the podium. "Are you going to say that?"

He shook his head. "What would be the point of insulting her to her friends, especially now she's dead?" He looked away. "There are better ways to honor her."

"Honor? But you hated her."

"She hated me. I felt nothing for her." With a humorless smile, he murmured, "I think that's what I liked most about her."

That didn't even make sense to Rosalie. But for the rest of the evening, as she watched him endure rudeness so calmly and politely, she marveled at his self-control. After the dinner dishes were finally cleared away, and the coffee poured, Giulia made a speech in Italian from the stage. Rosalie's eyes kept creeping toward Alex, as he watched with a faint smile on his lips, looking so handsome and powerful in his tuxedo.

He could have tossed this table, screamed, vowed to destroy everyone who insulted him. But he didn't. He showed restraint. He was a good man, she thought. And against her will, a tiny, stubborn thought crept through her brain, twisting and turning like a serpent until it was like a thick, unbreakable knot inside her soul.

She wished Alex was hers.

That she could have a husband that steady. That loyal. That honorable and kind.

Rosalie jolted out of her reverie when Giulia switched to English in her speech on the stage.

"And now, to accept the prize, is Chiara's husband—the Conte di Rialto! Who's even come here with his pregnant *friend*," she added spitefully.

Rosalie sucked in her breath, her cheeks burning red as her worst fear came true and a spotlight, indeed, did fall on their small table.

"Don't be shy," Giulia called. "Come up on stage, Alex, to accept Chiara's award!"

The ballroom fell silent as Alex stood up from the table and walked up the steps to the stage. Going to the podium, he put his large hands against it and spoke in English, looking out at the crowds.

"Thanks," he said with a casual smile. "I know Chiara valued the musical community in Venice. It's why she chose to live here. She valued Riccardo Carraro's genius above all." His voice was mild. Looking out at the crowd, he raised his voice. "And so, I have decided that my late wife's estate should go to support the musicians of Venice, with a million euros of it going directly to Carraro's wife—"

Total uproar took over the ballroom. Giulia, standing behind him, had a shocked, slack-jawed expression as Alex turned and took the small crystal "award" from her limp hands. Smiling, he kissed her on the cheek, as if to say *Checkmate*.

Coming down from the stage, it was a very different affair. People who'd glared and hissed earlier now stampeded over themselves to shake Alex's hand vigorously, thanking him for his generosity and telling him what a fine fellow he was, leaving Rosalie to wonder if it all, really, was only about money. It took some time for Alex to reach their tiny table. His dark eyes glinted as he held out his hand.

"Let's go."

Rising from her seat, Rosalie took his hand gratefully and let him lead her through the crowded ballroom. He didn't stop to speak to anyone, until a plump, dark-haired woman threw herself desperately into his path, pleading in Italian.

"Yes," Alex replied in English. "I meant it."

Looking at Rosalie, the woman switched to English. "Thank you. Thank you so much." She seemed near tears. "You don't know what this will do for us. My husband, he left no money, you see, and we have two young daughters—"

"Signora." His voice was gentle as he took the woman's hand. "I am glad to help you. My lawyer will contact you tomorrow. I wish you and your children well."

Then he pulled away, leaving her in grateful tears. Crowds of well-wishers started to gather around her as they left through the door.

Rosalie looked at him. "That was Carraro's widow?"

He shrugged. "She was innocent in all of this."

They left the building through a quiet side entrance, into the deepening night. She felt the welcome blast of cool air against her overheated skin. Above them, stars twinkled.

Alex didn't let go of her hand. They walked in silence down the slender sliver of Venetian alley. When they reached a deserted bridge crossing a dark canal, she stopped and looked at him.

"So you're just giving away Chiara's money."

"Yes."

"What about her land, where you've already invested so much time in the vineyard?"

"Ah. That's different." He gave a smile. "But even that, I will buy from her estate at a fair market price. And it will go to the musicians."

"Buy back something you already own..." she breathed. She shook her head, bewildered. "Why?"

Alex looked down at her. "Because I want to be free of her. Truly free. And it's the right thing to do."

Rosalie felt tears rising in her own eyes.

"You're driving me crazy, do you know that?" she choked out. "Why are you so amazing? Why are you everything I've ever wanted, everything I know I'll never have? It's not—"

But she cut off the last word, because Alex was right. Life wasn't fair. She should have learned that long ago.

She turned away, trying not to let him see her tears. Alex stopped her, roughly pulling her into his arms.

"But you do have me, Rosalie," he said huskily. "If you want me, I'm yours…"

And he lowered his head hungrily to hers.

His kiss was passionate, hard, full of desperate yearning that matched her own, as she clung to him on the moonlit Venice bridge.

When he finally pulled away, he said words she never imagined she'd hear from him in a million years.

"Marry me, Rosalie," he whispered.

Her lips parted in a gasp. "You said you'd never marry again…"

"I never intended to." Alex cupped her cheek. "But I want you in my life. Not just for a one-night stand. You are the mother of my child. I don't want you to find some other man. I want you to be mine. My wife. Now and forever."

Forever. Her heart turned in her chest. "But you don't…love me."

"Not like you've been dreaming of," he said

softly. "Our marriage won't be a fairy tale. Not like the poets say. But I want you, Rosalie. And I know you want me." He drew closer to her in the moonlight, pressing her hands against the white shirt of his tuxedo. "We can be good together. Raise our son together. We can be happy. Friends. Parents." He kissed one cheek, then the other. "Partners. In life." He ran his thumb slowly across her lower lip. "In bed."

Her body trembled at that touch. Her gaze fell unwillingly to his beautiful mouth as she heard herself whisper, "All right."

Alex blinked and pulled away. He looked down at her. "Think about what you're saying, Rosalie. Can you really be happy without a grand, romantic love? Because I take promises seriously. Happy or unhappy, marriage is forever. I'll never divorce you. Once we speak our vows, we're wed for life."

She swallowed. Her heart was pounding.

Was she making a terrible mistake? A corner of her soul was terrified and shrieking for her to slow down, to back away, to stop, to consider. But the rest of her just wanted Alex, at any cost. And that part was arguing even louder.

Rosalie wanted a real home, and knew she could never return to Emmetsville. She was tired of feeling sad and unsure about her future. *Put other people first if you want to be happy*, her mother had always said. How better to start than by putting their son first? And how better to do that than by marrying her baby's father?

For her whole life, she'd dreamed of having a loving marriage like her parents had. Wasn't that why she'd fled to San Francisco—because she hadn't been willing to settle for less?

But after her parents had died, everything changed. The light inside Rosalie had died. She was no longer sure she'd find that kind of love. No longer sure she even deserved it.

And so she'd agreed to be a surrogate. To help someone else. Because, in her soul, she'd given up hope.

How many times over the last year had she wished she'd married Cody Kowalski? Wishing she hadn't refused him because she'd wanted to wait for true love?

Her parents had paid the price for her selfishness. And if she refused Alex's proposal now, wouldn't she be doing the same to her baby? Holding out for some impossible dream of romantic love, that deep at her core, she no longer believed in?

We can be good together. Raise our son together. We can be happy. Friends. Parents. Partners.

Yes. Wasn't that what her baby deserved—a stable home and two parents living together not just for a few months but for always?

Partners. In life, he'd said huskily. *In bed.*

Rosalie shivered. It was the best offer she'd

ever had in her whole life. She wanted it more than anything. So why was she hesitating?

"I'm not a man who is comfortable sharing feelings," Alex said slowly. "I will never sing you love songs. If that is what you need—"

"It isn't." She didn't need love songs, Rosalie told herself desperately. She needed a home. She needed a partner. She needed a lover and friend. It would be enough—more than she deserved. She had to stop dreaming of some unreachable star. Alex wanted to marry her—wasn't that enough of a miracle? How could she possibly be greedy enough to cry out for more?

She was no longer a child, to believe in fairy tales, or expect life to be *fair*. She didn't need love. She didn't think she'd find it, anyway.

Reaching up her hand, Rosalie cupped his rough jawline. "I'll marry you, Alex."

With a rush of breath, he turned her palm to his lips and kissed it, causing electricity to sizzle up and down her body beneath the pink satin dress.

And as Alex pulled her into his arms, as he kissed her on the bridge, all her last doubts, all her soul's fearful cries, melted away like mist beneath the power and force of his hot, brilliant sun.

CHAPTER SEVEN

THREE WEEKS LATER, Rosalie held her breath as she looked at herself in the full-length mirror.

Her bridal gown was simple, a long white slip dress with a bias cut. The low-cut bodice, held up with spaghetti straps, caressed her full breasts and pregnant belly. Her long hair tumbled down her bare shoulders, crowned by a long translucent veil that stretched all the way to the floor, edged with lace. She looked like the perfect pregnant bride.

Except the face in the mirror looked scared.

The sweep of eyeliner accentuated her dark lashes above worried brown eyes. She'd already had to retouch her scarlet lipstick three times, because she kept biting her lips and smearing it.

How Rosalie wished she had someone here with her, to tell her she was doing the right thing in marrying Alex. If only her parents could be here, or childhood friends from back home. But the only person who might have come was Odette, and when she'd phoned her great-aunt to invite her to today's wedding, she hadn't exactly been reassuring.

"A wedding? So fast? What's the hurry?" her great-aunt had demanded.

Rosalie could hardly explain that her fiancé had refused to make love to her until their wedding night.

I cannot give you everything, but I can at least give you that dream, Alex had said, before kissing her until she was dizzy.

She could absolutely, positively never discuss *that* with her great-aunt. So she'd stammered, "We want to be married before our baby is born."

"That is when I will come visit," Odette had replied grandly. "In the autumn, when I can meet my great-great-nephew. *Zut*, that is a lot of *greats*," she muttered under her breath.

"But why wait? Why not come now? Alex can send his jet..."

"Oh, can he?" Odette had replied with asperity. "But he cannot cook my omelets or run my restaurant. I cannot leave Mont-Saint-Michel at the height of tourist season. We have yet to get a single bad review and I intend to keep it that way. Euros and good reviews, do you think they grow on trees?"

"Please, *Tatie*," Rosalie had whispered. "I need you."

Her great-aunt had paused. She said in a different voice, "You are sure about this marriage?"

"Of course," Rosalie said, putting every bit of certainty she could into her voice.

"Then *bon courage, ma petite*. And I will see you in September."

Courage and luck. Rosalie would need both today.

For the last three weeks, she and Alex had done everything legally required to wed. They'd procured documents, going to the American Consulate and the lower court, and waited for the banns. They'd signed a prenuptial agreement. At any moment, Rosalie had half expected that something would happen to stop the wedding, or that Alex might change his mind. But nothing had happened, and he hadn't.

Whenever she was with Alex, she was happy, her brain and body and heart all drugged with desire. Like last week, when he'd taken her to watch a glassblower on Murano. She'd watched the artist roll his fingers over the pole that he placed into the fire, twisting the glass into shapes at the end. She should have been paying attention to the creativity, to the artistry. Instead, she'd been distracted by Alex's powerful body sitting close to her own, and the glassblower's sensual dance of molten glass made her imagine what it would be like to have Alex's hands moving similarly over her body—over her breasts, her hips, her thighs...

She shivered, remembering.

It was only when she was alone, and it was

quiet, like now, that she felt the uncertainty in her heart whenever she remembered Alex's stark words.

Our marriage won't be a fairy tale. Not like the poets say.

And no matter how many times Rosalie repeated to herself that she wasn't a child and didn't believe in fairy tales anymore, she would remember her parents. They'd had such a loving marriage. Her father, early in the morning before he left on his tractor, had always started a pot of coffee for her mother, so it would be waiting when she woke. Her mother had responded by making his favorite dessert. And every evening, after dinner, her parents had danced to the old record player as they washed dishes together. Her dad would twirl Maman around the small kitchen, crooning old love songs by Bing Crosby and Nat "King" Cole. "La Vie en Rose" had been their particular favorite. Her father would sing it in English. Her mother would sing it in French. They would dance across the worn linoleum, with her mother's head pressed tenderly against his chest. Sometimes, they would see Rosalie watching, and they'd hold out their arms, pulling her into their tight circle of love.

Her heart hurt to remember.

I will never sing you love songs, Alex had told her. Looking at herself in the mirror, Rosalie suddenly couldn't breathe.

Was she making the worst mistake of her life?

There was a soft knock at the bedroom door.

"Cara?" She heard Alex's low voice as the door cracked open. "Are you ready?"

Was she?

Her heart was pounding.

She was doing the right thing, she told herself. She and Alex would be good partners and provide a loving home for their baby. She couldn't be selfish enough to hold out for romantic love, putting their baby's future at risk, especially when she no longer believed it would even happen. She took a deep breath.

"Yes. Come in." Leaving the mirror, she turned to face him. Pools of morning light from the high windows of the bedroom frosted her long bridal veil with gold.

Alex pushed open the door, then gasped when he saw her in the wedding dress. *"Rosalie."*

She looked at her future husband in the doorway. He was devastatingly handsome, his muscular body sheathed in a civilized tuxedo that masked the savagery of his powerful physique. But his face was awed as he slowly looked over her wedding dress, his gaze for once utterly devoid of mockery or cynicism.

Clearing his throat, Alex came forward, holding out a flat black velvet box. He opened it. "For you."

Rosalie's lips parted as he held up a beautiful

diamond tiara that sparkled and shimmered in the morning light.

"This has been in my family for generations." Setting down the black velvet box, he placed the tiara lightly on her head, crowning her tumbling dark hair and translucent white veil. Stepping back, he looked at her, his dark eyes warm. "Now it is yours."

Shocked, Rosalie looked back at the mirror. She hardly recognized herself, with her bold red lips and hair that looked almost black against the white gown. She looked like a princess. Reaching up, she touched the tiara with a trembling hand. The stones twinkled in the mirror, but felt hard and cold to the touch. "But—but what if I lose it?"

"The tiara is yours to keep or lose." Tilting his head, he said huskily, "I cannot wait to marry you."

Holding the tiara to her head, she ran to the bathroom and stuck in a bunch of bobby pins to hold it tight. With all the pins, and beneath the weight of the tiara, her scalp hurt, and her temples ached. Her heart was still pounding with fear for the commitment she was about to make.

A life with diamonds. But without love.

She would die without ever hearing a man tell her he loved her.

But how could it be a mistake, when it would allow their son to have two parents in a secure home…forever? How could it be a mistake, when it meant that tonight and for always, Rosalie would sleep in Alex's bed?

"Cara?" he said quietly. He held out his arm.

Her gaze fell on his antique cuff links, solid gold engraved with the Falconeri family crest. He had large, sensual hands, which she yearned to have on her body. His every teasing kiss, every passionate caress, made her burn until she thought she'd die. She had to marry him. *Had* to.

Picking up her bouquet of red roses, Rosalie placed her hand around his arm. He kissed her gently on the temple and led her downstairs.

They left his palazzo at the back, going to the private gate at the canal. She'd expected to see the speedboat. But instead…

"A *gondola*?" she gasped. He gave a sheepish grin.

"The speedboat left twenty minutes ago with decoys to draw away the paparazzi. Gondolas are only used by tourists. With luck, no one will even look at us."

As his burly-looking bodyguard, dressed as a gondolier, steered the picturesque boat down the canal, Rosalie looked out at Venice in the bright early morning. The golden rays of the sun burst over the water, gilding the edges of the streets, the alleyways peeking out from between the orange-and-red-stucco buildings. The Venice of dreams.

It was almost as good as a love song, Rosalie thought. A lump rose in her throat.

A light breeze blew against her bare shoulders, against her hot skin, causing her hair and translucent white veil to flutter behind her in the gondola. She gripped her small bouquet of blood-red roses.

"Cara?" Alex said incredulously. "Are you crying?"

She looked at him, blinking fast. She couldn't wipe her tears without wrecking her mascara. She tried to smile. "Of course I'm crying. It's our wedding day."

It was the most romantic moment of her life. The streets were still quiet, as it was early. To an observer, Rosalie probably looked like Cinderella getting whisked to a palace with a handsome prince.

But amidst all the beauty, all the glamour and romance, she knew what she was losing today, losing forever.

I have no choice, she told herself desperately.

Then she was tortured by the memory of Alex's earlier words.

There is always a choice.

She'd made hers, and she would have to forget about what she was losing today—the last hope of being truly loved. She didn't care. It wouldn't have happened anyway. She would wrap up her yearning in an iron box and dump it into the lagoon, never to be found again.

When they arrived at the palazzo where Venice's civil weddings were held, she kept her face frozen in a smile as Alex helped her out of the gondola and onto the dock.

His eyes were dark, his words simple.

"Are you sure?"

"I'm sure," she told him.

But was she?

Taking a deep breath, she went forward.

Inside the palace, Collins and Maria were waiting to be witnesses. Rosalie turned to Alex in surprise.

"You didn't invite your cousin, Cesare?"

"I changed my mind." Alex's expression became hard. "I barely know the man."

"But he's family!"

He shrugged. "He attended my last wedding, and it didn't help anything. Besides—" his hand tightened over hers "—you're my family now."

So their butler and cook would be their only witnesses. Rosalie wished her great-aunt could have been there. Or anyone from her hometown. Or most of all, her parents—

But thinking of her past only reminded her of everything she didn't want to remember. She lifted her chin.

"Maybe you're right," she said. "Let's keep the ceremony simple."

She turned to Collins and Maria, praying they wouldn't see her heart was crumpling inside her.

For my baby, she told herself, clutching the bouquet of red roses tightly. *For my baby.*

She flinched. Pulling back a hand from her bouquet, she saw a drop of blood on her finger. A single thorn, missed by the florist, had pricked through her skin.

"What is it?" Alex reached for her hand. Pulling a handkerchief out of his pocket, he wiped the blood from her finger. She looked at him in amazement as he tucked the handkerchief back into the pocket of his tuxedo jacket. A handkerchief? Was he from the nineteen hundreds?

Still holding her hand, he brought it to his lips. She felt the heat of his breath, the caress of his sensual lips as he kissed the back of her hand.

She shivered.

Desire. That was what they would have, instead of love. Longing and lust. As their eyes met, her fear was silenced beneath the pounding heartbeat of desire, like a drumbeat that drowned out everything else.

Desire. His hand tightened on hers, and he led her up the stairs of the grand palazzo. He didn't let go of her hand as they went into the small room where the official waited to marry them.

Rosalie barely listened to the Italian ceremony or the English translation. She didn't want to hear, didn't want to understand. All she had to do was make it to tonight. Then she'd let forever take care of itself.

Afterward, they signed the papers. An enormous diamond ring was added to Rosalie's left hand. They kissed. They stood. And suddenly, Maria and Collins were congratulating them.

Just like that, they were wed. All her worries no longer mattered. She was his wife. Now and forever.

As they left the building and went out into the sunlight, Alex took her left hand with its heavy new diamond. He cradled it against his powerful chest, and she held her breath as her bridegroom looked down at her.

"Well, wife," he said softly, "shall we go home?"

Before Rosalie could embarrass herself with a reply like *Yes, yes, yes*, or *Oh, please, yes*, Collins cleared his throat behind them. Alex looked back at the elderly butler. "Yes?"

"Your staff from the winery has a surprise for you, sir. They've rented out a nearby restaurant to celebrate your nuptials."

A flash of annoyance crossed Alex's face. "Tell them no."

"Of course." The butler bowed his head. "Though they've spent some time on it, sir."

Maria, the cook, added something in rapid Italian.

"Alex," Rosalie said. Putting off consummating their marriage was the last thing she wanted, but she could not imagine snubbing his employees after they'd made such an effort. "We can't be rude on our wedding day."

With a sigh, he said through gritted teeth, "It was very kind of them." He looked down the street. Crowds had started to form, holding up cameras, straining to see them. "It seems the world has already found us." He turned to Collins. "The reception is nearby?"

He pointed. "Across the bridge, signore."

"Make sure the bodyguards are close when we want to leave."

They walked the short way across the slender bridge to the party eagerly awaiting them in a local trattoria. Rosalie found herself engulfed by hugs and greetings as she met the employees and farmworkers from his vineyard.

"Welcome, *contessa*."

"So happy to meet you, *contessa*!"

Rosalie looked up at Alex in astonishment. "I'm—a countess?"

He encircled her with his arms. "That's how it works."

"Me!" An incredulous laugh bubbled up as she looked back at him. "A farm girl from Emmetsville—an Italian countess! How did I get so lucky?"

Alex kissed her.

"I'm the lucky one," he said huskily.

For lunch, they were served traditional Venetian dishes such as *caparossoi a scota deo*—

clams in lemon pepper—and *risi e bisi*—risotto with peas—at the long, rough wooden tables. Alex toasted his bride with champagne, holding out his flute and speaking in rapid Italian, translating his words into English for her benefit.

But Rosalie needed no translation. Sitting at the table of the trattoria, surrounded by new friends, she felt happy, from her fingertips to her toes, to be Alex's wife. She listened to the timbre of his voice, watched the movement of his body. Her gaze lingered on his large, capable hand holding the stem of the crystal flute. She watched his lips move as he spoke, noted the mesmerizing way they pressed together, lifted, laughed. Though it was only early afternoon, she noticed the five-o'clock shadow along his jawline, the thickness of his neck. As he took off his tuxedo jacket and rolled up the sleeves of his white shirt, her gaze lingered on his powerful forearms, laced with dark hair.

With his broad shoulders and muscular body, he seemed like a man who could lift a horse on his shoulders, or perhaps a car, or perhaps the whole world.

His low-slung trousers were trim against his slim waist. And as he turned to speak to someone who had come up to congratulate him, Rosalie's gaze fell to his backside, so taut and shapely beneath the fabric that her mouth went dry. As lovely as this reception was, she could hardly wait for it to be over. Because once they were alone, she would be able to see him. She would be able to *touch* him. She would be able to—

"Don't you think, *cara*?" Alex said, turning to face her, to include her in the conversation with his estate manager. Her cheeks went red as they waited for her reply.

"Um…yes—yes, of course," she stammered. Then, "Er…what?"

"I was saying we do not wish to post a wedding photo online, not even on the winery's social media accounts. Our celebration is private." He frowned at her, and she knew her behavior must seem strange; she must look like a fool. Then, looking at her more closely, Alex suddenly grinned, as if he knew exactly what she'd been thinking about—and liked it.

Her cheeks felt radioactive with heat. What was wrong with her? She was a virgin, but felt totally wanton, utterly in her husband's sexual thrall.

Her husband. Alex was her husband.

"Are you ready, *cara*?" he murmured hours later, holding out his hand as they finally left the trattoria.

This time, there was no hesitation in her answer, no doubt, no question. Looking up at him, she was vibrating with need.

"Yes," she said.

* * *

They took the speedboat back to the palazzo, going very fast to evade paparazzi hovering in their wake, and taking five wrong turns to throw them off the scent. Instead of going to the back gate on the canal as expected, Lorenzo dropped them at a dock a little way from the front of the palazzo. Taking Rosalie's hand, Alex led her down a tiny, winding alley, as they both laughed with joy at their escape.

Rosalie's heart pounded as she looked at her darkly handsome husband. When they reached the rarely used kitchen door of the palazzo, she was still laughing as she started to go through it. Alex stopped her.

"Wait," he said huskily.

Lifting her in his arms, he carried her over the threshold. She expected him to immediately put her down in the kitchen, because after all, at nearly eight months' pregnant, she wasn't exactly a waif. Instead, he carried her all the way through the kitchen, down the hall, into the grand foyer and up the stairs.

His footsteps never faltered. He carried her as if she were a feather.

Only when they were in his master bedroom, the room she'd never even been inside before, he slowly lowered her to her feet.

No. His bedroom no longer. *Theirs.*

Her eyes fell on the enormous four-poster bed,

and she bit her lip nervously. She was about to experience what all the fuss was about. She would make love to the man whose child she already carried…

They'd done everything backward, she thought suddenly. Getting pregnant. *Then* marrying. *Then* making love. The last thing should have been falling in love—because really, that should have come first, before anything else. But now it would come never.

This was close enough to love, Rosalie thought as he looked down at her, burning her with his hot gaze. It *was*.

Outside the windows, past the balcony, the sun was beginning to set, leaving a soft rose hue over the lush, warm Venetian buildings.

Reaching out, Alex pulled the diamond tiara slowly from her dark hair. As the pins disappeared, the long, translucent white veil, too, dropped to the floor. She shivered.

Cupping her face with his hands, Alex lowered his head and kissed her.

His lips burned hers, moving languorously, as if he had all the time in the world. His hands moved in her hair, stroking down her back. Her lips parted as he deepened the kiss, taking command, luring her tongue with his own.

Slowly, he unzipped the back of her wedding dress. It fell in a crumple of silk, gleaming on the marble floor with a pearlescent sheen. Pulling back, he looked down at her with wide eyes, his lips slightly parted.

The girl at the lingerie shop had practically forced her to buy this. "Perfect for a wedding night, *signorina*! It will make your *sposo* mad with desire!" That had sounded good to Rosalie, so she'd taken it, in spite of her blushes: a strapless white silk demi bra, which she saw now barely contained her overflowing, pregnancy-swollen breasts. Beneath her prominent belly, matching white silk panties clung to her hips. A white lace garter belt held up thigh-high sheer white stockings, which had seemed unnecessary in the warm Italian summer, but the salesgirl had insisted were absolutely necessary.

And now, looking at her bridegroom, Rosalie agreed. Because the expression on Alex's face was one so overwhelmed with shock and desire, it was almost comical.

"What," he breathed, "is that?"

"Lingerie," she said shyly, peeking at him. "Do you like it?"

With a low growl, he gripped her shoulders, pulling her into his arms, plundering her mouth with his own. A soft sigh came from the back of her throat as she wrapped her arms around him tightly, pulling him down against her.

He yanked off his tuxedo jacket, then dropped it to the floor. His antique cuff links came next. As he unbuttoned his shirt, she placed her hands against his bare chest, feeling the warmth of his skin over his powerful muscles, his flat belly, laced with dark hair. The shirt fell to the floor.

Gently, almost reverently, Alex lowered her to the bed.

Climbing beside her, where she reclined against the pillows, he kissed her. Slowly, softly, his hands caressed her, working his way down her body with the lingering stroke of his touch.

"My wife at last," he whispered huskily against her skin, and the words burned through her, nearly as much as his touch.

She wrapped her hands around him, exploring the muscles of his back, feeling the strength of his biceps as he cupped her full breasts over the tactile silk bra, running his thumbs over her taut, aching nipples. Moving the fabric aside, he stroked the sensitive reddish-pink tips with his fingertips. Her lips parted in a silent gasp as he touched where no man ever had before.

Reaching beneath her, he easily unhooked the clasp of her bra, and the white silk fell to the bed, fluttering like a flag of surrender. He bent his head, and she felt the heat of his breath, then the electricity of his lips on her nipple as he suckled her, drawing her deeply into his warm, wet mouth. She moaned aloud as pleasure crackled down the length of her body. Tension coiled low and deep in her belly.

He moved to her other breast, cupping the

weight with his large hand, squeezing it softly as he drew the large, aching nipple deeply into his mouth. She moaned again as he stroked her body. Lifting his head to plunder her lips, he ran his hands down her bare shoulders, through her hair tumbling over the pillow, then very gently over the swell of her pregnant belly.

Her hands traced the contours of his powerful chest, down his flat belly to the waistband of his tuxedo trousers. She felt the hardness of him beneath, pressing against her. He froze.

With an intake of breath, she looked up, her cheeks burning. "I… I don't know what I'm doing."

He cupped her cheek, his dark eyes burning through her. "You are wrong, *cara*," he said huskily. "You're driving me mad." Lowering his head, he kissed her naked shoulder, whispering against her skin, "Your every touch intoxicates me…"

Moving down her body, his fingertips lightly caressed her arms, her belly, to the edge of her white silk panties. They paused, then continued moving downward, to her hips, and her thighs beneath the white silk stockings. He unhooked the white lace garters, one by one, then slowly peeled the stockings like a whisper down her legs, first one, then the other. After he dropped them to the floor, he kissed the hollow of one foot, then the other. She shivered at the feel of his lips in that sensitive spot.

He moved slowly back up her legs, kissing as he traveled, and she felt the caress of his lips, of his hot breath, at the hollows of her knees, then her tender thighs, then higher still…

He unhooked her white bridal garter belt from around her waist. His hands moved over her silk panties, stroking over the fabric. Then he pulled those, too, slowly down her legs, tossing them aside.

She was finally naked on the bed. Her eyes squeezed tightly shut. Her breath came in sharp little gasps as he moved away from her. For the briefest moment, she felt nothing but cool air where the heat of his powerful body had been.

Then he lowered himself back against her. She felt his muscular legs, rough with dark hair, moving against her smooth ones, and she realized that he, too, was now naked.

"Rosalie."

She opened her eyes. His hard, handsome face looked down at her in the shadowy bedroom. His dark gaze burned her like fire. Stroking back her hair from her forehead, he gave her a wicked smile.

"You're mine," he whispered. He stroked down her full breasts, tweaking one of her taut, sensitive nipples, gently caressing her enormous belly. He kissed her forehead, her eyelids. He whispered against her trembling lips, "Every part of you belongs to me…"

Wonderingly, she stroked his bare chest. She marveled at the feel of him beneath her palm, his flat nipples, the tight muscles, like steel beneath satin. Her hand moved slowly downward, echoing his earlier exploration of her body. She traced the line of dark hair that arrowed down his flat belly, and down further still. She paused, then with a deep breath, she explored there, as well.

His shaft was rock hard, jutting from his body, enormous in length and width. She heard his quiet groan and hesitated. Then, with determination, she allowed her fingertips to caress the entire length, from the root to the bulbous tip, glistening with a single pearlescent drop. Curious, she wrapped her small hand around him, then stroked up, then down.

With a choked exclamation, he stopped her.

"What is it?" she said, pulling back her hand, looking up at him. "Do I not please you?"

"You please me too much." His deep voice was hoarse. "My bride. I want to make this last. I want to make your first time amazing. I want this to be…" He ran his hand through her dark hair. "The night we remember, as if it were the night we conceived our son…"

Lowering his body next to hers on the mattress, he kissed her slowly. His lips were hot velvet, as his tongue entwined with hers. She sighed as her lips parted in surrender.

His hand trailed lightly down her body as he brushed her shoulder, then cupped her breast. His hand stroked across her belly, then her hips. Pushing her thighs apart, he deliberately reached between her legs. She gasped as hc stroked her wet satin core with a fingertip, sliding against her, swirling.

Breaking their kiss, he moved abruptly downward. Kneeling between her legs on the bed, he lowered his head to where she could not see, beyond her pregnant belly. She felt his warm breath against her tender inner thighs.

Pushing her legs apart, he lowered his head. And he tasted her.

Pleasure exploded inside her. It was so intense, it made her hips shudder beneath him. He held her, swirling her with his tongue. Tremors exploded up and down her body. Her back curved off the bed as she held her breath, her eyes closed, her lips parted in a silent gasp.

His tongue was rough, lapping her with its full width, then softly, twirling her, feather soft with only the tip. Her whole body felt tight, arching off the bed once more as she exploded with a scream of ecstasy.

That cry was still ringing in her ears as he moved. Positioning his hips between her thighs, he pushed himself inside her in a single thrust.

She gasped, feeling him suddenly so deep inside her. Shockingly, new pleasure built, twisting around her, soaring her even higher, swirling around until she felt dizzy, whirled by a storm of intense pleasure. The hurricane buffeted her up, down, spinning her in circles, leaving her light-headed. He pushed inside her again, his whole hard length, moving slowly, so she felt every inch of him. As he filled her completely, she flew higher, and higher as he rode her, until her breaths came in soft desperate pants. She lost all awareness of identity, of time.

There was only pleasure. There was only *this*.

There was only him.

CHAPTER EIGHT

ALEX HAD NEVER felt like this before. He'd never known pleasure like this even existed.

He'd nearly exploded three times already. When he first took off her wedding dress. When he first touched her naked body. When he'd first felt her touch him, wrapping her hand around the length of his shaft.

But none of that had prepared him for this.

Pushing so deep inside her, he felt an intensity he'd never imagined. Though she was a virgin, there were no physical barriers, just the waves of pleasure he felt as he thrust deep into her tight, wet sheath.

He felt as if he, too, were a virgin.

But this was caused by more than just his long period of celibacy. Far more. It was as if he'd never even experienced sex before. Why? Was it because she was pregnant with his baby? Just seeing her swollen breasts and belly, and knowing she was ripening with his child? Was that what was causing such an overwhelming reaction inside him, body and soul?

No. It was more than even that.

It was *her.*

From the moment he'd first seen her, standing uncertainly in the salon of his palazzo last month, he'd hungered for Rosalie. For her beauty, her warmth, her light.

And now she was his. Truly and forever. She would be his until the end of time.

Just that thought caused a rush through his body. Holding himself up from her belly, with his hands pushed against the bed, he thrust inside her a second time, even deeper, and groaned. Pleasure swirled around him in crashing waves, making him struggle for breath. He pushed inside her again, and again, knowing he was on the razor-thin margin of control, barely keeping himself from exploding.

Then he heard his wife cry out with new ecstasy, felt her tighten around him as her fingernails pressed into his skin. He held himself still, his eyes squeezed shut, battling to hold himself back. He wanted to last, damn it. He wanted to bring her to fulfillment not just twice, but an infinite number of times. He wanted their wedding night to last in this moment of pure joy…

But even as he had the thought, he knew he could not endure for much longer. Her hips undulated beneath him. He was so close—

Abruptly, he rolled off her, onto the bed. Her eyes opened, but before she could ask the question he saw forming in her mind, he lifted her, carefully placing her on top of him.

For a moment, she hesitated, and he thought she might refuse to take the lead, that she might be too shy in her inexperience. Then she took a breath, and, watching his face, she lowered herself deliberately, drawing him deeply inside her.

But that was when it really fell apart.

He'd thought being in this position might make it easier, might help him hold on to his shreds of self-control. But as he looked up at his bride leaning over him on the bed, as her breasts swayed over her pregnant belly, he gave a choked gasp. She rode him, slowly at first, then quickly building up speed. Her lips parted, her expression fervent, almost glowing, illuminated by the soft light of the Venice night.

Looking up at her beautiful face, he saw her eyes had closed with a new intensity as she rode him harder and faster, gripping his shoulders tight, pushing herself against him, harder, deeper—

She screamed, even louder than the two times before. An answering growl rose from deep in his throat. Feeling dizzy, he gripped the bed beneath him with white-knuckled hands to keep himself from flying up into the sky. She pushed down harder, pulling him more deeply inside her as his growl built into a hoarse scream echoing and crashing against the walls of the bedroom—

He exploded, as his soul shattered and broke into a thousand chiming shards.

Alex was only dimly aware of her falling beside him on the bed, exhausted. Only dimly aware of cuddling her beautiful, sweaty body, pulling her back against his chest in a tangle of limbs, hardly knowing where she ended and he began.

Afterward, he only gradually came back to awareness. He remembered where he was. In the palazzo. Who he was. Alex. When he was. His wedding night.

He tenderly kissed his wife's temple. Her eyes were closed, her breathing even. She was asleep, he thought. As well she should be. He'd never felt so spent—as if every drop of him had been wrung dry. He had nothing left.

Or so he thought. Until about ten minutes later, when, feeling her delectably round backside nestled naked against his groin, to his shock he started to stir again. Even as a teenager he'd never felt like this, so full of endless hunger and need. For Rosalie. His wife. *Forever.*

Brushing back her dark hair, Alex kissed her cheek, then nuzzled her ear. He nibbled the tender corner between her neck and shoulder. With a delicious sigh, she turned to him, wrapping her arms around his neck as her eyes fluttered open. He felt her glorious naked breasts pressing against his chest, thrusting upward toward his chin. In devoted obedience to their demand, he lowered his head in worship, cupping their magnificent weight in his hands, lifting a full, red nipple to his lips. Tugging it into his mouth, he felt the soft, sensual tip pebble against his tongue, as he suckled her, until he felt her body rise with sweet new desire.

Then he lifted her leg up over his hip, and he took her right there, pushing himself deeply inside her, filling her every inch. Fulfilling her every need. He heard her gasp as she gripped his shoulders, straining against him, pressing harder, deeper. He squeezed his eyes shut as she filled his senses, his soul, his every dream. She was his.

And he was hers.

The next morning, when Alex woke in the magnificent bedroom of his Venice palazzo, he looked down at Rosalie, curled up in his arms beneath the soft rose-gold light.

How was it possible that she'd come a virgin to his bed? He still didn't understand such a miracle.

She'd saved herself for love.

The treasonous whisper went through him with a stab of guilt.

No, Alex told himself firmly. She'd saved herself for *marriage.* She'd given up the ideal of love, for the sake of a stable home for their baby, companionship and passion. And he would give all those things to her. She would never have cause to regret her choice.

And as he kissed her bare shoulder, incredibly he felt himself stir yet again, even after all their lovemaking the previous night. With a soft sigh, Rosalie woke, turning in his arms to say shyly, "Good morning."

"Good morning." Her smile was so beautiful that it made his throat ache. Leaning forward, he kissed her lips, her cheeks, her forehead as he murmured, "I can hardly believe you're mine, that some other man didn't marry you before now."

Her expression changed, and Alex wished he hadn't brought it up. Both of them were still naked in bed, facing each other. And yet a wall suddenly separated them. She looked away.

"Someone proposed to me once. The boy who lived at the farm next door. My parents were thrilled." Her voice was quiet. "But I didn't love him, so I refused."

"I understand," he said, thinking of Chiara and how he'd married her for her acreage. He reached for her, intending to change the subject with a kiss.

She pressed her hand against his naked chest, stopping him. "No. You don't. It wasn't just my parents who thought Cody and I would marry. It was everyone in Emmetsville. We'd dated in high school. We were perfect for each other. He said he loved me. He proposed. But—"

"But?"

"I never felt like I thought I should feel." She looked away. "My parents were shocked. Everyone asked how I could refuse him, when he was so perfect for me, when he loved me so much. I couldn't take it. So I left. I moved to San Francisco, to be a receptionist, and live with strangers."

"You did what you had to do," he said gently. His hands tightened as he thought how grateful he was that she hadn't married some farmer in California. "It was fate—"

"No," she whispered. She suddenly wiped her eyes. "It was selfishness. I should have been there for them."

"Rosalie."

"No," she choked out. She sat up in bed. "My parents died because of me. If I'd done what everyone expected me to do, they would still be alive now—"

Her voice broke on a sob. Sitting up on the bed, Alex pulled her to his chest without a word. As she cried, he stroked her hair, her back, murmuring soft words in Italian. He stroked her until the sobs subsided, until there were no tears left, falling cold against his bare skin.

Outside the balcony window in the fresh air of morning, he could hear the distant cry of gulls, the sound of a speedboat on the canal and a low buzz of voices. Apparently the tourists were out early.

Rosalie felt good, too good, in Alex's arms.

"How can you say it was your fault, Rosalie?" he asked in a low voice. "How could it be?"

"If I'd been there, I would have insisted my parents leave town immediately, at first word of the wildfire. I would have forced them into the car and driven them out of the valley before the fire picked up speed and crushed both sides of the road." She wiped her eyes in a rough, jerky movement. "But I wasn't there. I abandoned them, just because I didn't love Cody and..." She turned away. "I was selfish. Evil."

Stroking her hair, Alex said in a gentle voice, "Seeking your own happiness doesn't make you evil."

She shook her head wildly, her eyes glistening in the morning light. "My parents made the wrong choices without me. They tried to pack their things, they waited too long, until there was no escape. *Cody* managed to get his parents out. *They* lived. My parents...they died."

Her voice choked off as she looked away.

Alex could hear the anguished love and loss in her voice. "It wasn't your fault."

"But—"

He kissed her cheeks, her forehead. "Your parents loved you, Rosalie," he whispered. "They never would have wanted you to suffer. You did nothing wrong. It wasn't your fault."

He held her, comforting her, until he finally felt her relax in his arms, pressing her cheek against his shoulder. Then Rosalie looked up, her stunning brown eyes swimming in tears. "You know how it feels."

He gave a single nod. "I lost my family too." Even to his own ears, his voice was cold. "My older brother and parents died at Christmas." Looking at the tears still glistening in her eyes, he forced himself to go on. "I'd promised to go home. But I couldn't face their yelling and screaming. So they decided to take a ski trip instead, and crashed into a mountain." He paused. "The jet I took to their funeral…it was my last one. After that, I suddenly couldn't stand the sight of a plane, any plane, big or small." He looked away. "And that was before birds flew into the engine of my sister's plane in Chile. A plane she wouldn't have been on if I'd gone to Boston in her place."

His throat was so tight he couldn't say more.

"No wonder you're afraid of flying," Rosalie murmured.

"Yes," he said quietly. "I'm afraid." He wondered if she had any idea how much that admission cost him. It was something he'd never said out loud before. "I lost them. All of them."

"But the crashes weren't your fault." She put

her hand on his cheek. "They were accidents. Tragedies. Why can't you believe that?"

Looking at her, he said in a low voice, "Why can't you believe that about the wildfire?"

For a moment, they looked at each other, cuddled so close together on the bed.

Dropping her hand, Rosalie said, "But your cousin—"

"*Second* cousin," he corrected.

She scowled. "Why do you insist on doing that?"

"What?"

"Emphasizing that he's a distant cousin. Pushing him away." She shook her head, her beautiful face puzzled. "Is he such a horrible person?"

"No," he was forced to admit.

"A liar? A thief?"

"No."

"Then it's his family you don't like. His wife?"

Alex paused. He hadn't thought too hard about why he avoided Cesare. He still didn't want to think about it. But with his wife looking at him, in the early-morning light, he wanted to please her. He wanted to distract her with anything that wasn't forcing him to explain how he'd destroyed his own family. He scrambled to think of a reason that might satisfy her about Cesare.

"It's complicated" was the best he could come up with.

She waited. Alex tried to think of something else, but his mind was unhelpfully blank.

"I already told you why I didn't invite him to our wedding," he said irritably. "He'd been to my first one. There was no point in inviting him to another."

Rosalie stared at him incredulously. "That doesn't make any sense."

No, it didn't, and he didn't want to explore it further. "Rosalie, *cara*, I don't want to fight." Pulling her into his arms, he nuzzled her close. "It's our honeymoon, and..."

"What's that noise?" she asked, turning away.

Alex realized the low buzz of noise he'd noticed earlier had built to a roar. It sounded like a vaporetto with a fully gunned motor. Rising from the bed, he looked out at the small canal, three stories below. He saw a few boats, hanging out conspicuously near his private gate.

"Paparazzi," he said grimly. "On boats."

"They're making all that noise?"

Still naked, he padded to the opposite window in the corner bedroom. Looking downward and to the right, he could just barely see into the square.

There, he saw people with cameras, reporters, all shoved into the tiny square, as if ten cruise ships had dumped all their passengers on the doorstep of his palazzo. As if his life were a mere entertainment for others.

"Oh, no." Rosalie stood beside him, her body

wrapped in a sheet. Her face was almost that same color as she looked up at him. "What do they want from us?"

"A story," he replied, his jaw tight. He looked at her. "I'm sorry. Paparazzi have been following me for years, because my parents were well-known, but especially since Chiara's death. And now, with social media...and the new story about a mysterious pregnant woman, and now our wedding...they're more voracious than ever."

She looked panicked. "We're trapped. Prisoners."

Alex glanced out at the crowds. It was worse than ever. But the truth was, he'd put up with being a story for a long time. He'd thought he didn't have a choice. For years, Alex had told himself he didn't care. His strategy had been to hide out at his vineyard and ignore everyone and everything.

But Rosalie couldn't. She cared too much about other people to ignore them. She had no protection against this kind of onslaught. He hated the fear he saw on her face. It was even worse than tears.

"We're not trapped," he said grimly. "We're leaving. Now."

And so it was that, four hours later, they were driving toward his country villa outside the city in a vintage blue Fiat.

It hadn't been easy to escape from the palazzo

unnoticed. They'd had to enlist not just Alex's two regular bodyguards, but the men's girlfriends as decoy versions of Rosalie, to lead the paparazzi away on two separate merry goose chases via speedboats on the canal. An hour later, their housekeeper and butler had staged themselves in the top bedroom window of the palazzo, moving like shadows to deceive the remaining crowds, while Alex and Rosalie crept out the side door, hunched beneath drab brown coats.

But now, they were finally free. Rosalie sighed happily as Alex stomped down on the gas of the tiny two-seater car, zipping through the Italian countryside.

"I can't believe you even own a car like this, that can actually blend in!" she said with a big smile.

"This is Maria's car." He grinned. "I asked for a loan, but she says it was a straight-up trade and she's permanently keeping my Lamborghini." He paused. "She probably deserves it, after all that time pretending to embrace Collins behind the window."

Rosalie gave a low laugh, running her hand along his shoulder. Her warm brown eyes danced as she looked at him. Her dark hair was tucked back behind a jaunty yellow scarf, and she wore a white cotton sundress in the heat of the Italian summer. He felt her happiness and an answering lift in his heart. Then her fingertips brushed his neck, the tender flesh of his earlobe, and he felt a different sort of lift slightly lower down.

"Don't do that," he said.

"Why? You're my husband. I own you."

He growled, "You'll make me pull over and take you right now."

"In this tiny car?" She gave a low laugh that sounded impossibly sensual. Her dark eyes challenged him. "I'd like to see you try it."

Put like that, Alex had no choice. He abruptly pulled over on the side of the road, where he kissed her until they steamed the insides of the windows. Then he discovered to his regret that his wife had been correct. There was no good way to make love in a two-seater car. Luckily Collins had packed a picnic lunch in the back before they made their escape from Venice.

Finding a quiet spot on a lonely lane, Alex parked the car behind a copse of trees. Lifting the picnic basket to his shoulder, he led her to a small clearing on the gentle incline of the hill. Spreading the blanket on the soft grass, he kissed her until she was trembling with need. He made love to her right there, pulling off her panties from beneath her dress, unzipping his trousers and lifting her on top of him on the blanket, until she gasped and screamed, and so did he, with only the birds to hear them.

Afterward, once they'd recovered, they had a delicious lunch of antipasto, sandwiches and sparkling water. Then, refreshed, they drove the rest of the way to his estate.

"That's it," Alex said finally, pointing.

"That?" she said in awe, looking at endless hills all covered with vines, beneath a wide blue sky with gray clouds in the far distance. As they drove past the vineyard's gate, where he nodded at the guard, Rosalie looked out at row after row of vines, stretching as far as the eye could see. "It's beautiful."

"I'm glad you like it." He smiled at her. "Chiara hated it here. She wanted to sell it from the beginning."

"Did you get her land sorted out?"

"I spent an exorbitant amount to purchase it, yes. The musicians of Venice will be dining on lobster and champagne for quite some time."

Rosalie looked forward, then saw the elaborate, gracious villa, surrounded at a distance by the outbuildings of the winery. Her eyes were huge in the dappled light as she turned back to him. "That's the house?"

"It is."

She bit her lip. "But it seems so…quiet. Where do you hold wine tastings? Where do the tour buses park, so people can visit your winery's fancy restaurants and art galleries and…?"

"I don't have any of those things." He remembered that she'd come from Sonoma, famous for its own wineries. So she knew how they worked.

"You should see what some of the other wineries around here do. Offer tourists hot air balloon rides. Golf. Climbing walls and goat yoga. Trying to sell as many bottles as possible."

"What do you do?"

"Nothing."

"Nothing?"

Alex shrugged. "I'm not trying to build a fortune. I already have one. All I care about is making wine. I let it speak for itself, no gimmicks, and produce only a limited number of bottles. La Tesora is my private home. Tourists are not welcome here."

Rosalie gave a laugh. "I guess that explains the marketing strategy of the big no-trespassing sign at the gate."

"We don't even advertise."

"So where do people buy your wine?"

He gave a low laugh. "Anywhere but here."

When they finally pulled in front of the villa, he helped her out of the car as two smiling employees, whom she'd met at her reception the day before, whisked away their bags. Taking her hand, Alex led her toward the entrance of the sprawling, elegant villa. Her eyes were huge as she tilted back her head.

"It's so grand," she breathed.

"It looks old, doesn't it? But my great-great-grandfather built it for his wife in 1905. It was meant to evoke the romance and drama of the eighteenth century, only with the modern comforts of plumbing and hallways. I've added other things too. Technology. Solar paneling. There's a few people you haven't met yet. Gabriele," he called. "Come meet my wife."

Several older men with rumpled clothing and ready smiles came over and introduced themselves shyly, touching their caps as they spoke to her in Italian. She spoke to them in English, but somehow everyone got along just fine.

She glanced back at Alex, her eyes dancing. She was so beautiful in this moment, with her white sundress—a bit wrinkled by their interlude on the hillside—and bright yellow scarf in her hair, that he impulsively took her in his arms and kissed her.

When Alex finally drew back, he saw his employees glancing at each other with raised eyebrows. They clearly thought their boss had lost his mind. But he didn't care.

In the distance across the vineyard, the dark clouds in the far sky came closer as a summer thunderstorm approached.

Rosalie drew back from his embrace, looking up at him with flushed cheeks. The emotion in her deep brown eyes pierced his heart. He felt an answering flash sizzle through his soul like lightning, but he pushed it away. Desire, this was desire, nothing more. As he lowered his head back to hers, he buried all other emotions, walling off his heart. And he ignored the low roll of thunder trembling the earth beneath his feet.

CHAPTER NINE

SUMMER PASSED SWIFTLY in Veneto, one of the largest wine-growing areas in Italy, rivaling the more famous regions of Tuscany and Chianti. As June turned into July, then August, the weather was invariably sunny and hot; with the buzzing of bees in the golden light as in the vineyard, the grapes grew.

Rosalie, too, grew riper in the warm sun. Each day, she felt more relaxed, strolling lazily in the hot sun, as her belly expanded until she felt bigger, yet more contented, than she ever had before.

She'd never had such a wonderful summer. As Alex had promised, there was no one to bother them here. No paparazzi, no cruise ships, no tourists. Each day, Alex put on his work clothes—here, jeans and a T-shirt, not a bespoke suit—and got his hands dirty, toiling alongside his farm workers.

The very first day, when Rosalie had appeared at his side to walk his rounds, similarly dressed in pregnancy overalls and a white T-shirt, her hair bound up in a ponytail, ready to work, he'd been astonished.

"You forget—I'm a farm girl," she'd said with a smug grin, pleased to surprise *him* for a change.

Nine months before, when she'd conceived this baby via surrogacy in San Francisco, she could never, ever have imagined a life this wonderful was in her future. She'd thought then that she'd be lonely and grief stricken forever. She'd never dreamed she could be this happy.

Now as the three-wheeled Ape truck took them out to the edges of the estate, she put her hand over her forehead, blocking the sun from her eyes, and felt her whole body relax beneath the warm hazy light.

She'd forgotten how much she missed this, being out on the land. For two years, she'd been cooped up in an office in the big city. She was comfortable here as she hadn't been in San Francisco, or even in glamorous Venice. She *liked* wearing farm overalls. This was so much like her childhood. So much like home. So much like before—

Rosalie caught the thought in its tracks, shoving it away before it could clutch at her heart.

No. She wasn't going to think of the past anymore, only the future. She looked at her husband, driving the two-seater pickup truck beside her. Everything had changed. Their baby was due any day now.

In the last few weeks, she'd learned so much, living in a new country, meeting new friends. But farm life had felt somewhat familiar, at least, and she'd started to learn Italian, thanks to daily lessons arranged by the villa's housekeeper.

"You feel this land," Alex said, watching her as she walked through the even lines of growing vines. Stopping, she looked at him.

"I love this place," she said honestly. "It's almost like home."

Almost. Her family had raised crops like alfalfa and melons. She still didn't know much about viticulture or *vendemmia*, the autumn wine harvest. But she could only go forward, not back. She'd try to accept this new country as her own.

She'd never think of what she'd left behind. Never.

With a sudden frown, Alex tilted his head. "Should you be walking so much?"

"Waddling, more like," she sighed.

Coming closer, her husband pulled her into his arms. "You've never looked more beautiful."

Rosalie let him hold her, accepting his comfort and warmth. She was already three days past her due date. Her Venice doctor had been temporarily lured to a small private hospital nearby, at an exorbitant rate. The doctor was checking on her daily now. If Rosalie didn't go into labor soon, she'd been warned she might need to be induced, which sounded like no fun at all. To be honest, nothing about labor sounded terribly fun. Except the end, when she'd finally hold their baby in her arms.

Pulling away, she gave her husband a rueful grin. "Walking is good for me. Dr. Rossi said exercise might help me go into labor."

Lifting a dark eyebrow, Alex looked down at her wickedly. "She suggested other things that might help too."

She snorted a laugh. "You can't mean—"

Cupping her face with his hands, he lowered his lips passionately to hers. His embrace was fierce as his strong arms wrapped around her tenderly. When she finally pulled away, she looked up at his handsome face in wonder.

Warm golden sunlight was bathing the countryside, making it glow. And it gilded Alex most of all. He looked so handsome, gazing down at her, almost as if he—

As if he—

No. Rosalie couldn't let herself believe it. Just the thought caused a twinge deep inside her.

"Let's go back to the villa," he whispered, running his hand suggestively down her back.

"In the middle of the day?"

"Why not?"

"Gabriele and the rest would be shocked if—"

But as she turned to walk away through the vines, she felt the hard twinge again, and a moment later, she sensed it a third time. There was an ache in her lower back that she'd been ignoring all day. She suddenly realized what it was. She stopped in the middle of the row. She turned back to him with an intake of breath, her eyes wide, holding her belly.

Alex looked at her face. She didn't have to say a word. He rushed to her, scooping her up in his arms.

"I can walk," she tried to tell him, but he was implacable.

"No, *cara*," he said gently. "Let me help where I can."

Rosalie thought of the upcoming labor and was terrified of the unknown, the pain, everything she'd have to go through before she could hold her baby. "Promise you'll stay with me."

Alex's gaze went straight to her heart. "I promise."

Rosalie knew what a promise meant to him. Looking into her husband's face, held by his steady, powerful arms, she was suddenly no longer afraid.

Alex had just witnessed a miracle.

Sitting in a private suite of the small, modern hospital, he looked down at his newborn baby son in awe.

Tiny. So tiny. He looked at the minute fingers. He'd arranged for the DNA test, as a matter of form. He trusted Rosalie completely, but he'd wanted to make sure the California clinic hadn't made some mistake. But now, even with the baby's scrunched-up face, he saw the exact resemblance to his own baby pictures.

For so long, Alex had dreamed of having a child to carry on the family name. And now it had happened at last. He had an heir.

But it wasn't just an heir. This was a living, breathing child. His heart pounded as he looked down at his son.

Sitting in a soft chair by the window overlooking the lush Italian countryside, Alex had been shirtless for the last twenty minutes. When the baby had started whimpering and crying, the nurse had recommended that Alex comfort him with skin-to-skin contact. Pressed against his father's warm chest, cuddled beneath a blanket, the baby had swiftly quieted, then fallen asleep.

Alex looked at his wife, who was sleeping in the bed. He thought of everything she'd gone through to give birth. The pain, the fear. It had been a long night. He'd been at her side the whole time, ordering ice chips, raging at her doctor to do something, anything to ease her agony.

"It is too late," the doctor had replied crisply. "The baby is coming too quickly."

"I can deal with the pain," Rosalie had panted, her forehead sweaty, her eyes glazed. "Please, Alex. Just stay with me."

She'd reached out her hand. He'd taken it. He'd held it for two hours.

Now, he stretched out his hand ruefully. His bones seemed to creak. He could still feel the bruises.

But how proud he was of her. He was in awe of her courage and strength. He didn't know if he could ever endure what she just had.

And now, the room was quiet. Both his wife and son slept. Their breathing was even and soft, the sweetest music he'd ever heard.

Alex looked around the private hospital suite. The light from the window was golden, just as it had been yesterday, when he'd kissed her in the vineyard. The room was filled with bouquets of flowers, sent by his acquaintances from around the world, and by the estate staff, who already loved her.

Somehow, this summer had been the best time of his life. He'd never imagined any marriage could be so…happy. Not something to be endured, but actually enjoyed. And not just at night, when they set the world on fire, but during the day too. Rosalie had become not just his companion, but his friend. His true partner.

As he held his newborn, whom they'd named Oliver Ernst Falconeri after Rosalie's father, Alex looked across the room at his sleeping wife. And the emotion in his heart was so strong he almost couldn't bear it.

It was too much. He couldn't care this much. His heart started to race, going faster and faster. He couldn't have this much to lose. If he failed them—

So much could happen. To this tiny, fragile baby. To his tender, openhearted wife. How could he prevent any possible disaster? How could he keep them safe? His hands tightened around the sleeping bundle in his arms.

Alex had never felt like this before. Certainly not with Chiara. Marrying his first wife had been easy. Without passion, without love, there'd been no fear, no jealousy, no heartbreak, just coldness—his own personal Antarctica, right here in Italy.

His own childhood had been full of drama as his father argued hatefully, always going for the jugular, and his mother gave them all the silent treatment for days, both of them forcing their children to endure the endless cycle of misery. His older brother, Thomas, had soaked up their malice like a sponge, and learned to fight with the same weapons. They'd still died, and so had his sister, though she'd tried to flee and start a new life. And look at Rosalie's parents—they'd died in a fire.

Anything could happen, at any age, even to people who were rich. Even to people who were loved. Even to people who were good. There was no safety net. He could lose Rosalie. They could lose their child.

Alex suddenly felt dizzy. He took a deep breath, trying to control the frantic pounding of his heart.

He couldn't let anything happen to either of them. He had to hold it all together. To be tough. To be strong. To be steel.

He couldn't let his emotions take over, leaving him afraid and weak, with his heart pounding like this, his breath a shallow gasp, and all from fear. Knowing his wife and child could be taken from him at any point. Knowing they could die.

Knowing they could leave.

A man was only as good as his strength. As good as his promises. Alex had to protect his family. And himself.

The only way to keep them all safe was to stay vigilant. To stay strong. To imprison his feelings, chaining them beneath walls of iron, chiseling them beneath stone.

He took a deep breath, forcing his heart to ice.

The only way to love his family…was to not let himself feel anything for them at all.

For the first few weeks after Oliver was born, Rosalie's days and nights blended into a haze of waking and sleeping.

She was tired, so tired. Her nipples were sore from nursing. Her shoulders ached from holding her newborn baby in the same position for hours as he slept, afraid of waking him, as she herself dozed upright in the rocking chair.

"We should get a nanny," her husband had told her multiple times, every time he saw her drugged-looking expression and the dark circles beneath her eyes. "A night nurse, at the very least."

But Rosalie had refused. This was her precious baby, and he deserved all her attention and love. She held him for hours, both because he cried when she set him down and also because she wanted to. She cradled his warm, tiny body close to her chest, and breathed in the scent of him, baby powder and sweet skin. Her baby needed her more than anyone ever had.

Oliver's birth utterly and completely changed her life. In more ways than one.

Labor had been difficult, especially since she'd been forced to do it without an epidural. For hours, she'd endured the worst physical pain of her life. She didn't know how she would have gotten through it if she hadn't been able to grip Alex's hand. "I'm here, *cara*," he'd murmured softly, his dark eyes glowing. "I'm here."

Afterward, exhausted, she'd cuddled her sweet newborn, and then slept. But when she'd woken, she had opened her eyes and had seen everything she'd ever dreamed of.

There, on the cushioned chair beside the window of the private suite, Alex sat cuddling their tiny baby.

He was shirtless, holding their son against his powerful, tanned chest, rippled with muscle and laced with dark hair. Both of them were half-covered by a knitted baby blanket sent overnight by her great-aunt from France.

And it was in that moment, buried beneath an avalanche of emotions, that Rosalie suddenly realized what she really felt.

She was in love with her husband.

All summer, she'd denied her growing feelings. They were merely partners, both in the vineyard, and as parents-to-be. Yes, they were lovers, and every night he brought her to shuddering, gasping fulfillment.

But that didn't mean they were *in love.* Even though he'd become her best friend, the person she kissed before she fell asleep at night, the one who made her smile when she opened her eyes each morning. The man she wanted to spend time with; the one she wanted to talk to. But that didn't mean she loved him. Of course it didn't.

But when she saw him holding their baby son, her heart had simply exploded. And she could no longer deny the feeling or pretend it was anything else.

She was in love with Alex.

Totally, recklessly and utterly in love.

It terrified her. She tried not to think what it

could mean for their future. Love had never been part of the deal. In fact, when she'd married him, he'd warned her: there would be no love. And there would be no divorce.

After they'd left the hospital and returned to the villa, she'd been almost relieved that, in those very early days of motherhood, she'd had no time to think about it.

But now, with Oliver nearly two months old and sleeping in four-hour chunks at night, she'd slowly resurfaced from the haze. Coming up from the baby undertow, Rosalie's brain began to function again. And she was forced to face the cold, hard fact of her love.

And she was afraid.

Because now, for the first time, she also saw how her husband had grown increasingly distant since Oliver was born, spending very little time with them. Her husband never volunteered to care for their baby. In fact, after that miraculous afternoon in the hospital when he'd cradled him to his bare chest, he'd barely held his son at all.

It was almost, Rosalie thought with a shiver, as if he was purposefully trying to push her away. As if he *knew.*

But he couldn't know she'd fallen in love with him, she told herself desperately. His emotional distance had to be a coincidence. When she'd been busy, utterly focused on the baby, exhausted and barely surviving, she hadn't asked him for help. And in fairness, he'd been nearly as busy himself, with harvest. Harvesting grapes was labor-intensive, as Alex still insisted on the traditional method, harvesting by hand, with sharp shears and baskets. So it was all hands on deck. Alex always paid the top wages in the game, so he had no problem finding employees, and he himself worked hardest of all, from dawn till dusk, harvesting first the white grapes, mostly pinot grigio, and now the red, pinot nero and merlot.

An entire season of growing could be undone if the grapes were harvested too soon, or too late. So it was an intense, stressful season, until the grapes were all safely harvested and brought to the winery on the estate, where they'd be sorted, destemmed and crushed. Harvest was the most important time of a vintner's year.

That had to be the reason he seemed so distant now, so hostile almost, whenever Rosalie tried to speak to him. She hadn't even been able to tell him about the latest offer she'd received from a corporate American winery, asking to buy her family farm.

If she was truly never going back to California, she should sell, rather than continue to pay taxes on land that was going to seed, left a fallow ruin. The town deserved better. But every time she tried to force herself to accept the generous offer, she couldn't. She couldn't face it alone.

But Alex never talked to her. They hadn't

shared a single meal together since the baby was born. She tried not to take it personally. But it was hard. Especially since they hadn't made love since the baby was born. They'd been separated not just by day, but by night too.

At first, after her difficult labor, and exhausted and zombielike from lack of sleep, sex had been the last thing on Rosalie's mind. She'd even moved out of their bedroom to sleep on a cot in the baby's nursery. She was waking up so continually with the baby; it seemed cruel to disturb Alex's sleep, as well. After all, *he* wasn't able to take catnaps with the baby throughout the day, but had to go out into the vineyard to put in fourteen-plus hours of hard physical labor.

But now Rosalie was getting more sleep, and she'd been given the all clear by her doctor two weeks ago, after her six-week checkup. But she was still sleeping alone in the nursery.

Her great-aunt Odette, who'd arrived three days earlier for her long-promised visit to see the baby, had looked at the lonely cot in the nursery and said, "Are you a single mother now, *ma petite*?"

"No, we're married, of course I'm not!"

"Then why are you sleeping alone?"

Rosalie had blushed. "I've been busy, and so has he…"

Odette had narrowed her eyes, looking intently

up at her niece, then shaken her head with derision. “You must change this, Rosalie.”

“I don’t know how.”

“You simply go back to his bed.”

“I’m…” Swallowing hard, she’d admitted quietly, “I’m not sure if he wants me there.”

Her great-aunt’s dark eyes had glinted. “Then you should find out.”

Find out. Right. It should have been the easiest thing in the world. All Rosalie had to do was ask her husband if he still wanted her.

Except she was afraid she already knew the answer. He hadn’t so much as kissed her since their baby was born, beyond an occasional disinterested peck on the cheek.

“I can’t,” Rosalie had whispered. She half expected Odette to offer a scornful response. Instead, her great-aunt put a gentle hand on her arm.

“When you’re stuck, Rosalie, the only way to move forward is to change. Take a risk. Be bold.”

Thinking about it now, as she walked through the long downstairs hallway of the villa with her baby on her hip, Rosalie was wistful.

Take a risk. Be bold.

Easy for her Aunt Odette to say. She’d never been afraid of anything. But Rosalie—

How could she just climb back into her husband’s bed, when for two months, he hadn’t touched her? When they’d barely spoken? They’d become like two strangers, living in the same house. When she had news to share, she sent him a text.

Her aunt was right, she thought in horror. What had happened to their marriage?

But at least tonight, harvest would end. It was the final night of *vendemmia*, with the last grapes picked. At dusk, all the workers would celebrate by gathering around a bonfire, indulging in a feast, telling stories and polishing off last year's wine.

Take a risk. Be bold.

Maybe she could find a way to—

"Contessa, there is a phone call for your husband," called the housekeeper anxiously.

"He is out in the fields..."

"*Sì*, but the man says the *conte* does not return his calls, and it is urgent. Would you speak with him, *per favore*?" Rosalie hesitated until the housekeeper added, "He says he is his cousin."

"His cousin!" Rosalie brightened. "Of course I will speak with him!"

Propping Oliver against her hip, she reached for the house line in the kitchen. Cesare Falconeri did not seem surprised when Rosalie introduced herself as Alex's wife.

"Yes," the man replied. "My wife told me Alex was married. She read about you online. And I've heard you have a child?"

"Yes." She smiled down at her tiny baby, who was making *ba-ba-ba* sounds. "His name is Oliver."

"We are leaving for London next week and won't be back until spring. My wife has been dropping hints that we should visit you and drop off your wedding gift."

"You didn't need to get us a gift," she said, blushing. Cesare laughed.

"You don't know my wife, obviously, or you'd know that isn't true."

"I'm sorry we didn't invite you to the wedding…"

"You don't need to explain." And Rosalie got the feeling that she really didn't—that he understood. As she exhaled in relief, he continued, "But we'd love to see you now. I've been leaving my cousin messages for the last few days, but he hasn't responded."

"Alex has been busy with harvest," she said awkwardly, embarrassed.

"Oh, yes, of course—I should have remembered. Perhaps it's not a good time. You could come visit us in London this winter…" His voice sounded doubtful, as well it should. Rosalie couldn't imagine Alex traveling all the way to London when he couldn't be bothered to visit them here. "Or we could arrange for our families to meet in spring? By then, we'll have another one." Cesare's voice was fond. "Our fourth."

"Fourth!" she gasped, astonished.

"I'd like my other three to meet their new baby cousin. Not to mention you and Alex."

"Your kids have never met Alex? That's ridiculous!" She looked down at her own baby, who desperately needed cousins. Her child had so little family. So did she.

Take a risk. Be bold.

"I have an idea," Rosalie heard herself say. "Tonight is the last night of harvest, and we're having a bonfire with all his employees and staff to celebrate with dinner and wine. Why don't you join us?"

"Are you sure Alex would want us there?"

"Of course I'm sure," she lied stoutly. "After all, it's a party! Please come at eight, if that's not too late for your family."

"Wonderful. We'll make sure the children take a nap beforehand. We look forward to it. *Grazie mille*, Rosalie. And thank you." He paused, and added, "Oh, and my wife wants me to tell you her name is Emma, and she can't wait to meet you, because the wives of Falconeri men need to stick together. I can't believe you made me say that," she heard him grumble affectionately to his wife as he hung up.

Smiling, Rosalie put her baby down for a nap and took a long, hot shower. Afterward, she looked at herself in the mirror. Her great-aunt was right. She was already feeling more hopeful. All she needed to do was be brave enough to make some changes. How hard could that be?

Instead of her usual jeans and T-shirt, she

reached into her closet for a red dress she'd never worn before. It was a soft knit fabric, forgiving of the few pounds of baby weight she had yet to lose, while flattering her curves. The scarlet fabric looked striking against her dark hair, which tonight, instead of pulling into a ponytail, she let tumble over her shoulders, brushing it until it shone.

Tonight, things would change, she vowed. They'd come together as a family. She and Alex would finally reconnect. Now that he was done with harvest, he could wake up from his trance, as she had. He'd take her in his arms and kiss her, really kiss her. She'd be back in his bed tonight.

Maybe, if she was really brave, tonight at the bonfire she could even tell Alex she loved him. Rosalie looked at herself in the mirror.

Maybe not.

But everything was going to be fine. So she was in love with her husband. That wasn't such a disaster, surely? They had so much to be grateful for. A good harvest. A happy, healthy baby. Long-lost family coming to visit. What could possibly go wrong?

CHAPTER TEN

THE BONFIRE LIT up the autumn night as wine flowed from oak casks and tables groaned beneath enormous bowls of pasta, antipasto and freshly baked bread, as well as luscious desserts. Laughter ran through the small crowds of farmworkers, winery staff and house staff, all of them gathered together in a raucous, joyful celebration of a bountiful grape harvest. *Vendemmia* had come early this year, at the very end of September, after the hot summer.

Rosalie had been nervous when Cesare, Emma and their three children had arrived at the villa earlier that evening. Alex was still out in the fields; he had no idea she'd invited his cousin's family to their home. But she'd discovered, talking to the villa's housekeeper, that Cesare wasn't just a billionaire hotel tycoon, but also a prince.

She'd been briefly nervous, wondering if the Falconeris would scorn her. But as soon as Rosalie welcomed them into the library, she'd swiftly realized she had no reason to be scared.

"Me, scorn you?" Emma said later, after Rosalie confessed her fear. "Why would I ever do that?" She gave a low laugh. "Don't you know I used to be a maid at Cesare's hotel?"

When Rosalie met them, she discovered Cesare was tall and dark, with the Falconeri good looks, in his midforties with streaks of gray at his temples. His American wife was lovely and kind, perhaps in her midthirties. She'd immediately given Rosalie a big hug and put her at ease with a warm smile. "So you're Rosalie! I'm so happy to meet you at last. And this is your baby?"

"Oliver," she'd replied, holding her yawning child close. "He's nearly two months old."

"Adorable," Emma sighed, stroking his dark tufts of hair. Then she'd looked back at her own brood with an impish grin. "And these are our little monsters. That's Sam—" she motioned toward a studious dark-haired eight-year-old poring through the leather-bound books on the library's shelves "—and Elena—" a pouting little girl who was vigorously thumping her older brother with her teddy bear "—and Hayes—" a toddler who was frantically pulling on the shirts of both his elder siblings. Emma put her hand on her belly, which only had the slightest curve. "And there's this angel, due next spring."

Rosalie looked at her in amazement. Emma Falconeri seemed so calm and put-together, so effortlessly chic and lovely, while for the last two months, contessa or not, Rosalie had felt like a zombie in yoga pants with baby spit-up on her shoulder. Today was the first day in ages that Rosalie had felt like herself, rather than just a baby accessory. In her flowy red dress and red lipstick, she almost felt pretty. But she had only one child, while Emma had nearly four. She blurted out, "How do you manage?"

Smiling at her children, Emma looked back at her handsome husband fondly. "With help."

Coming close to his wife, Cesare took her in his arms and kissed her tenderly. "Nothing makes me happier."

The way Cesare looked at his wife…

Rosalie's throat suddenly hurt.

"Well, come on," she told them finally. "Alex is outside. The party has just started. He will be surprised to see you!"

"Surprised?" Cesare's dark eyebrows lifted.

"Happy," Rosalie amended quickly.

Alex was surprised, all right. But he wasn't happy. After a brief stop to introduce the Falconeris to her great-aunt Odette, who'd decided to skip the party in favor of a good book and glass of cognac by the fire in her room, Rosalie led the family outside. Still holding her yawning baby, she went out into the field between the villa and the winery, where the bonfire was being held, beside fairy lights and a few heaters in the rapidly cooling evening.

Her husband's dark eyes widened when he saw Rosalie in the red dress. His sensual lips curved and he started to come toward her.

Then he saw Cesare, Emma and their children behind her. And from his expression, Rosalie suddenly knew, with a chilling certainty, that she'd made a horrible mistake.

"Look who's come to visit," she said lamely.

"I see." Alex looked at her, then at his cousin. "How did it happen?"

She lifted her chin almost defiantly. "I invited them."

"Ah."

"It seemed past time for our children to meet."

"Of course." Reaching out, Alex shook his cousin's hand, asking Cesare how he was, as if it had been merely days since they'd met, rather than years. He then politely extended his hand to Emma, who pushed it aside to give him a warm hug.

"It's good to see you again. I'm sorry we missed—" Pulling back, Emma finished awkwardly "—so much."

So much, indeed, Rosalie thought. They'd missed their wedding, and for all these months, though living so close, they'd never even spoken.

The Falconeri children, after dutifully saying hello to their baby cousin Oliver, ran off to look more closely at the bonfire—and more important, the food table—as their father shouted a warning,

"Don't break anything," and their mother called with a smile, "Be careful, cuties, stay close."

"So…how are you, Alex?" Cesare said.

"Fine," he snapped.

Three pairs of adult eyes turned on him in amazement.

Alex added politely, "The grape harvest was excellent. The hail did no damage."

"That's good." Cesare cleared his throat. "The hotel business has been solid. We now facilitate owner-operated homestays, for those who want a different kind of luxury experience."

Silence fell. Their two wives glanced at each other with chagrin.

"I need to feed Oliver and put him to bed," Rosalie said. "I'll be back in a bit…"

"I need to keep an eye on my children," Emma said. "With all the farm equipment around, you never know when Elena might try to convince one of her brothers to jump into a vat…"

The two women's eyes met, then they deliberately left the Falconeri men alone.

But forty minutes later, after Rosalie tucked her sleeping baby into his crib, leaving Odette to listen to the baby monitor, she went back outside, only to find the Falconeri men on opposite sides of the bonfire, still not talking.

"Did you and your cousin have a fight?" she asked Alex. He turned on her, the fire leaving a red flicker in his dark eyes.

"He's my *second* cousin."

"Why do you always insist on adding that? What difference does it make?"

"You shouldn't have invited them here, Rosalie."

"They're your family," she said stubbornly.

"Like I've told you before—just because they're family doesn't mean they're not strangers."

"That's ridiculous." When he didn't answer, she demanded, "Why are you being so rude?"

"If I'm rude, it's your fault," he replied coldly. "I never invited them here. You did. So you can entertain them. Excuse me. I have work to do."

And Alex left her standing alone on the edge of the bonfire, as he stomped into the winery across the field.

So Rosalie spent the next hour talking to his employees, thanking them for all their hard work, and trying to entertain the Falconeris in such a way that they wouldn't notice Alex's incredible rudeness. The party started to wind down, as people wandered half-drunkenly back to the village or the staff quarters behind the villa. Finally, Cesare came to Rosalie by the dying bonfire.

"Thank you for inviting us," he said quietly. "We should go."

The Falconeri children were all yawning, and the toddler, Hayes, was actively crying, being comforted by his mother, who, being newly pregnant, looked rather tired herself.

Looking at them, Rosalie suddenly felt like crying too. This wasn't how she'd thought the evening would go.

Holding her two-year-old on her hip, Emma came to them. "Thank you, Rosalie. It was fun."

"No, it wasn't," Rosalie said, wiping her eyes. "I'm sorry. I don't know why Alex…"

"Don't worry about it," Cesare said. But it was obvious he was a little affronted by his cousin's coldness.

"Well, meeting you and the baby was fun, at least," Emma added cheerfully.

"And I got to spend the evening with you." Cesare looked at his dark-haired wife. "Every moment with you is pure pleasure."

"*Every* moment?" Emma said teasingly, glancing at her tired toddler and bickering children.

"Yes. Every one." Pulling her close, Cesare then kissed her softly on the lips. Rosalie saw the love in their eyes as they pulled apart, the two of them so obviously crazy about each other, even after three, almost four children and many years of marriage.

Looking at them made Rosalie's heart hurt. She would have given anything to have her own husband look at her with that kind of love in his eyes.

But he didn't. Instead, for the last two months, Alex had barely glanced at her at all.

Rosalie shivered in the deepening autumn night. She suddenly felt very cold.

"Here, I'll take him," Cesare said to Emma, lifting the toddler to his shoulder, where the boy laid his head to rest with a snuffle. "Good night, cousin," he told Rosalie, smiling, as his wife gave her one last hug.

"We'll see you again soon."

With many farewells and promises to meet in the future, the family left. For a long moment, Rosalie stared after them, her heart yearning. That was exactly what she wanted. A large, noisy family. A loving marriage. That was happiness.

Could she ever have that?

She didn't know if she deserved it, after the way she'd abandoned her parents. But whether deserved it or not, Rosalie wanted it. So badly it made her heart ache and swell until pain was all she felt and all she was.

And suddenly, she clearly saw the truth of her great-aunt's words.

The only way to change everything was to risk everything. To be brave enough to speak the truth from her heart.

As the bonfire died down to embers, after the employees had all left, Rosalie went to where her husband was putting out what remained of the flames. Reaching out her hand, she put it on his shoulder.

Alex looked at her coldly. His handsome face was half-hidden in the shadows of the fading firelight.

"What is really going on?" she asked quietly.

He looked down at the last embers and ash. His hands tightened. "Cesare and I have nothing in common. There's no reason for us to be friends."

"And us?" She lifted her gaze to his. "Is there any reason for us to be friends?"

Frowning, he straightened, still holding on tightly to the water hose. "We aren't friends. We're married."

"Yes. Married." With a deep breath, she forced herself to be brave. "I've missed you, Alex. Talking to you. Sleeping beside you—and all the rest of it. What's happened to us?"

For a moment, his dark eyes looked haunted. Then his jaw tightened, and he looked away. "Nothing."

Take a risk, her great-aunt had said. *Be bold.*

"Well, something's changed for me." Rosalie took a deep breath. "I'm in love with you, Alex."

Alex stared at her in shock.

A ripple went through his body, a seismic tremble, causing his heart to shake.

Rosalie loved him? How could she love him?

His knees felt weak. He staggered back a single step as he looked at her.

Her brown eyes were bright beneath the moonlight. A cool autumn wind mussed her long dark hair, blowing against her red dress, moving the knit fabric sensually against her small waist and legs. Her lips were parted. She seemed to be holding her breath.

She loved him.

Shock waves reverberated through him, sinew and bone. He wasn't worthy of her love. He didn't have the ability to love her back.

"Rosalie," he began hoarsely. Then he stopped.

"Yes?"

Seeing his wife's beautiful face turned up to his so hopefully, so bravely, he felt sick. The last thing he wanted to do was hurt her. It was one of the reasons he'd kept his distance. He had to protect her.

And he had to protect himself. He couldn't weaken. Not now. Not ever.

As he put out the final flames of the bonfire and watched the last embers die, Alex felt rising despair. He couldn't love her—couldn't she see that? He had to be tough and strong to be able to keep his promise to protect them.

But how could he say that without hurting her?

Rosalie waited silently with tortured hope. Then, slowly, her expression changed. He saw disappointment. Then pain.

Soon her love would turn to hate. Their marriage, their lives, would be destroyed. Along with their child's—

Fear pounded through him, surging like rain.

He'd somehow known this would happen, from the first moment he'd seen Cesare's family tonight. His distant cousin was, to all appearances, utterly lost in playing his sickeningly sweet role of devoted family man, as his wife clung to him like he was Christmas and joy and heaven all wrapped into one.

But their dream world couldn't last. Soon—or perhaps even already, behind closed doors—his second cousin's marriage would dissolve into screams and accusations. And their three innocent children would be the ones to pay the price. They would suffer for their parents' love. As everyone suffered, if they believed romantic love could actually *endure*.

"I love you," Rosalie said again, helplessly.

Alex's shoulders sagged. He looked down at his hands. The last embers of the bonfire were gone. He pushed through the ashes with the tip of his boot to make doubly sure.

Turning away silently, he walked back to the barn with the hose and turned off the water. He took a deep breath. Gripping his hands at his sides, he walked back to her. He found her by the villa, beneath the windows. She turned, her body visibly shaking as he stopped her.

"I'm sorry, *cara*," he said in a low voice. He had to force himself to look at her. "I'm just not made that way."

Her face started to crumple. She took a deep

breath, looking gorgeous in her red dress, her tumbling hair streaked with moonlight.

"I can be patient," she said. "I can give you time—"

"No," Alex said savagely. He had everything he'd ever wanted. A son to carry on his name. A beautiful wife who loved this land as much as he did. A partner. A friend. But it had come at a price. "It can't happen."

"I can wait." Coming forward, she put her arms around him. He stiffened, his heart pounding as he felt her soft body against his own. Standing on her tiptoes, she pressed her cheek to his, whispering once more against his skin, "I love you."

Every time she said those three little words, it felt like a gut punch.

He drew back from her almost angrily.

"Stop it, Rosalie. I told you from the beginning. I can't. And you agreed to marry me anyway. You agreed!"

"I know." She closed her eyes. He saw the single tear falling down her cheek, heard the tremble in her voice. He blocked a rush of emotion from his heart.

"You made your decision." His voice was hard. "You can't go back on it now, or ask for more than I can give. It's not fair."

Looking up at him, she tried to smile. "Weren't you the one who told me life isn't fair?"

She looked pitiful, in spite of her lush beauty.

Begging for his love. He hated himself. The villa that had been their home looked dark behind her, dark and empty and cold.

"You made your bed," he told her coldly. "Now you must lie in it."

A light went out of her eyes. He couldn't bear it. Urgently, he yanked her into his arms, searching her gaze.

"I can give you anything else you desire, Rosalie. Diamonds. Yachts. Palaces. More children." Cupping her cheek, he looked down at her fiercely. "We can be happy enough. If you'll just let us..."

He lowered his lips to hers, trying desperately to burn through her love, to crush it to dust, to leave it in ashes like the bonfire. *Passion.* It was the one thing that had never failed them. For the last two months, he'd tried to keep himself distant, because he was afraid of his own feelings. But now, he feared something more—he feared hers.

He tried to deepen the kiss, pushing her lips apart, plundering her mouth with his tongue. He wanted to prove to her that a loveless marriage didn't mean a sexless one, and could be very pleasurable indeed. He tried to entice her, to punish her, to force her to match his fire. She always had.

But for the first time, her lips were strangely lifeless beneath his. Pain gutted him that he couldn't control. He ripped away from her.

"I can't love you or anyone." His voice was a frustrated shout in the darkness. "Why can't you accept it?"

"I have." Her voice was dead.

"Why can't you be happy, like you were?"

"Because—" She looked away. "I want more."

Alex stared at her. Taking a deep breath, he looked down, gripping his hands at his sides.

"I know you're scared," she whispered. "So am I."

"You don't know what you're asking."

"I know the risk." Rosalie met his gaze. "I know the cost."

Angry, defensive words rose to his lips, his usual defensive mechanism, to be sarcastic, to be cold, to create distance. Then he looked at her, remembering her pain over her parents' deaths.

He said in a low tone, "Love doesn't last. It only leads to anger, to yelling and coldness and hate."

"With Chiara?"

"I never loved her. She was safe. But my parents. They used to yell and scream and—I've seen it too many times, with everyone I know. However happy Cesare and his wife look now, it will end that way with them too. Love always ends. Either in hatred, or in death."

Reaching out, she grabbed his hand. "You're right. Life ends in death. Hatred is optional. So is love. But if we're afraid to feel either one, what are we left with except emptiness? What is that, but killing ourselves while we're still alive?"

For a moment, Alex felt the magnetic pull of her, of the emotional longing in her lovely brown eyes. All he had to do was surrender. All he had to do was give in—

But if he let himself feel, thirty-five years of repressed emotion might swallow him whole, drown him.

He looked away. "I can't be like you. Perhaps you can love like that. I cannot. I don't have the capacity. I never learned how."

"That's not true. If you'd only—"

"I can't," Alex cut her off. "I'm sorry." He exhaled, then looked down at her. He repeated in a low voice, "I'm sorry."

"All right." With an intake of breath, she tried to smile, even while her eyes were luminous with unshed tears. "I'll try to live without it."

Without love? Alex looked at her beautiful yet miserable face.

Could she? And could he let her do it?

CHAPTER ELEVEN

"YOU'VE BECOME A DOORMAT, *ma chérie*."

The next morning, after Rosalie had stumbled out of the small cot in the nursery, exhausted from a night tossing and turning and getting up twice to feed the baby, she came downstairs with Oliver to see if the housekeeper had made coffee. She looked out the windows and saw bright sunlight pouring over golden fields and clusters of trees in vivid autumn reds and oranges.

So beautiful it hurt.

She found Odette alone in the kitchen. The white-haired Frenchwoman handed Rosalie a steaming china cup of coffee laden with sugar and cream. But as she breathed her gratitude and took her first sip, her great-aunt had said those words that burned through her heart.

Swallowing hard, she looked down at her baby prattling happily against her hip.

"I'm not a doormat," Rosalie told them both.

Odette shook her head. "You look like you need something for strength. I'm making you an omelet." Pulling down a copper pan from a hook, before whisking eggs and then adding ingredients, her aunt said, "Last night, I had my window open. For fresh air."

Rosalie swallowed. "What did you hear?"

Her aunt met her gaze. "I heard my precious niece beg for the love of her husband, and accept it meekly when he refused her."

Rosalie blushed, horrified. Setting the china cup down on the counter, she said in a low voice, "What else can I do? Alex is right. He told me from the beginning he could not love me."

"Why did you marry him, then?"

Rosalie gaped. "You were the one who said I should!"

"I said your baby needed a stable home and father," the older woman corrected. "I never said you had to marry him."

Hadn't she? Rosalie struggled to remember.

Odette looked at baby Oliver, with his chubby cheeks and good nature. "Do you want your son to grow up thinking this is normal in a marriage? That he should have no feelings and ignore his wife and child?"

Rosalie sucked in her breath. "I cannot force Alex to love me. So what choice do I have?"

"Plenty."

"I made my bed—I must lie in it," she said, echoing her husband's words.

Her great-aunt gave a low curse in French that made her blush.

"Tatie!" Rosalie said, scandalized.

"You made your bed, *oui*. But you can change the sheets. You can sleep on the sofa. You can decide not to sleep. You have many choices." Her dark eyes gleamed beneath the wrinkles as she placed the hot omelet on a china plate in front of her. "But what you must not do is sleep on a cot in your child's room, accepting a sexless marriage, or crawl back in surrender to your husband's bed, accepting a loveless one."

"He'll never divorce me."

"Who is speaking of divorce?" As Rosalie ate the omelet, her great-aunt tilted her head. "You told me you received another offer for your land in Sonoma. A very generous one."

"Yes," she muttered as she ate. She still hated the thought of selling her parents' land. But she couldn't just abandon it forever, lying fallow and forlorn. "They want an answer. I need to decide, one way or the other."

"Go home," Odette told her firmly.

Finishing the delicious omelet, Rosalie realized she'd been hungrier than she'd thought. "You want me to come back with you to Mont-Saint-Michel? I'm not sure if I could…"

"No. Home." Her great-aunt looked at her. "California."

Go home?

A whoosh of fear went through Rosalie, making her light-headed.

Odette put her wrinkled hand over hers and said very gently, "It's time.

It was an uncharacteristic display of sentimentality for her fierce great-aunt, and one that Rosalie was still thinking about two hours later, after Odette had departed in a chauffeured Rolls-Royce on her scheduled return to France.

Her aunt had only been at the villa for a few days, but immediately, Rosalie missed her. She felt more alone than she had since her parents had died.

Go home, her aunt had said.

Could she? Could she finally face it?

The last time she'd been to Emmetsville had been for her parents' funeral. She'd tried to erase that from her memory. The smell of ash in the air. The blurs of anguished faces. The sound of crying, including her own. And worst of all, the awful thump as dirt hit the coffin lids. Her parents had been buried together, for eternity, leaving Rosalie alone.

Cody Kowalski, the neighbor who'd once asked to marry her, had tried to approach her at the graveside service. He'd started to say something, then stopped, red faced. Stammering, *I'm so sorry*, he'd simply fled.

But Cody didn't need to say anything. Rosalie's guilt filled in the blanks. If she'd married him, if she'd stayed in town, she could have saved her parents, as he'd saved his.

Even after all this time, the thought was radioactive inside her.

While the baby took his early-afternoon nap, Rosalie went into the empty study inside the villa. It was a very masculine room, with wood and black leather. Sitting at the dark wood desk, she drew out her laptop computer from the bottom shelf. After opening it, she reread the email from the California corporation offering to buy her family's land. She should just accept it. They'd send a check to Italy, and she'd never have to go back. Never have to face her fear.

Her fingers hovered over the keyboard.

Alex came into the study. "Where have you been? I was..." Then he saw her stricken face. "What's wrong?"

Heart pounding, she looked up at him. "I need to go home."

His face shut down. "This is your home."

She shook her head. "I've had another offer for my parents' land."

"So?"

"I've been putting off the decision."

"You don't have to do anything."

"But I do," she whispered over the lump in her throat. She glanced out the window toward the lush Italian countryside. "Everything you feel about this vineyard—I feel the same about our farm. My family's lived there for a hundred years. And Wildemer just offered me a fortune for it."

"Wildemer!" He scowled at the name, one of the largest wineries in the world. "Don't sell to them. You don't need the money." He paused. "I would suggest we build a vineyard there ourselves, but this business is too personal to me." He gave a humorless laugh. "I could hardly oversee a vineyard in California, traveling by ship and train."

"Of course not." But suddenly, Rosalie wished they could. If Alex was with her, she thought she could face anything. Replant. Regrow. Rebuild.

She shook her head, shaking the foolish dream from her mind, along with her dream that her husband could ever love her. How many fantasies must she have, and all of them doomed to fail? She took a deep breath.

"If I never intend to go back, I must sell. I can't just leave it a ruin. It's not fair to the town, or to my parents' memory." She looked back at her computer, then squared her shoulders. "I must go."

"To California?"

"I have been hiding from this too long. I have to face it, for the baby's sake." She looked up from the desk. "If I can't be brave, how can I teach Oliver to be?"

Alex was looking at her strangely in the slanted light from the blinds.

Rosalie swallowed. "Will you…" She hesitated, then said in a rush, "Will you come with me?"

If he came with her, she wouldn't be so scared. She could hold his hand, until she got through it, like she had when she'd given birth to their son.

Glancing away, her husband said softly, "I can't."

"We could take a ship—"

His face was like stone. "*No*, Rosalie."

Her heart cracked as her last hope faded. "You really don't care at all, do you?" she said slowly.

He didn't meet her eyes. She thought of his earlier words: *Just because someone is family, doesn't mean they can't also be strangers.* He'd meant it, she realized. Every word. And it was killing her.

Rosalie was his family now. She was his wife. But to Alex, she'd always be a stranger.

She was utterly, completely alone.

Looking at her in the shadows of the villa's study, Alex couldn't bear the pain in his wife's eyes.

You really don't care at all, do you?

If only she knew!

Ever since his son had been born, he'd done everything he could to keep his distance from Rosalie, not just emotionally, but physically. Even after the doctor had given her the all clear, he'd stayed away. He'd feared, if he made love to her, he would surrender. Afraid he'd fall apart.

If he gave in to weakness, gave in to his feelings, then how would he defend against the decades of repressed pain he'd barely kept at bay? He'd end up sobbing in some corner, totally useless to anyone. Now more than ever, he needed to be strong for his wife and child.

So he'd tried to stay in control, cold as ice. He'd tried as hard as he could to keep his promise to take care of Rosalie and their son.

Alex had done everything he could to make her happy. But since last night, when she'd outright begged for his love, he'd realized how completely he'd failed.

She'd asked for his time and attention, and he'd refused. She'd asked for his love, and he'd refused. Finally, today, she'd asked for him to come to California with her. To be her comfort, her shield. It was a simple enough request. It should have been easy.

But even that, he could not do.

Rosalie was counting on him for strength and protection. How could he show her all the ways he was less brave, less strong than she?

His word was all he had. All of Alex's family had died—because of him. Because Alex had broken his word.

But now, he suddenly realized that Chiara had died because he'd *kept* it.

What did that mean? He put his hand against

his forehead as his brain whirled. And then he suddenly knew.

There was no protection. There was no defense. No matter what Alex did, he destroyed anyone who got too close.

Rosalie and the baby would be better off without him.

It was a cold, ruthless thought. But though it filled him with despair, he could not argue with its truth.

All this time, he'd been so determined to keep his promises, as a means of saving his broken soul. But he'd been living in a dream.

He'd already broken his word to Rosalie. He'd promised to care for her. He'd promised she'd never regret marrying him. He hadn't. And she did. He looked at her.

"Go to California," he said hoarsely.

"All right," she said softly, not meeting his eyes.

All right, as if it meant nothing. Just as she'd said it last night, when he'd told her he'd never love her back. Simple as that. *All right.*

"And don't come back," he heard himself say.

She blinked, rising slowly from the desk. "What?"

Once, nothing had been more important to Alex than vows. Than honor.

But if he forced her to stay in this marriage, as he'd done with Chiara, then sooner or later, he'd ruin Rosalie's life—and their child's. Just like he'd ruined everyone else's.

He couldn't be that kind of monster.

"My jet will take you to California immediately," he said in a low voice. She couldn't know how much even that cost him. Allow her and the baby on a plane?

But then, Chiara had died in a car. It wasn't the means of transportation that ruined people's lives. It was being close to Alex.

Rosalie looked confused. "What do you mean, don't come back? It's only for a few days. Will you be joining us in California?"

"No." His throat hurt. He couldn't destroy her. He had to let her go.

"I don't understand."

"I don't want you here anymore. Neither you nor the baby." Alex took a deep breath, clenching his hands at his sides. Looking straight into her beautiful, warm, loving eyes, he said in an expressionless voice, "I want a divorce."

Divorce?

Rosalie recoiled. It was the one thing she'd never, ever expected Alex to say. The man who'd absolutely refused to divorce his first wife, even when the woman had blatantly cheated on him in public, wanted to divorce Rosalie, who'd done nothing but support and love him?

She staggered back as the world collapsed beneath her feet. Their marriage was the one thing she'd assumed she could count on. No matter what.

"What about *happy or unhappy, marriage is forever*?" she choked out.

"I changed my mind," he said flatly.

"And our baby?"

For a moment, Alex didn't speak. Then he said in a low voice, "We'll come to some custody arrangement."

Rosalie could barely breathe. "I don't want that."

Alex stared at her coldly. His hard jaw was tight, and so was his posture. Every inch of his powerful body seemed about to snap. "Too bad. Because I do."

She wasn't going to beg. She *wasn't*. She'd done enough of that last night at the bonfire. She wasn't going to—

"Please, Alex," she heard herself say in a small voice. "Whatever the problem is, we can work through this. We have to stay together—"

His dark eyes looked through her as if she were a stranger. "I cannot be what you need me to be."

"Just try." Rosalie felt like the lights and shadows of the study were spinning around her in a whirl. She felt like she was drowning in tears. "We can go to counseling. We can—"

"No."

"People can change. Just look at what I'm doing now. The thing I'm scared of most. I'm going home."

"Yes. You are." His voice was hard, yielding nothing.

"Please don't make me do this alone," she said, and she didn't just mean her trip to California. "Come with us."

He drew back, clenching his hands. Then he shook his head. "You're better off without me."

Rosalie didn't want a divorce. As unhappy as she'd been lately, giving up on her marriage was the last thing she wanted to do.

But neither could she be the way Alex had been, when he'd coldly refused to set his first wife free. If Alex wanted this divorce—so much he was willing to sacrifice his honor and the sanctity of his promise—then Rosalie had no choice but to give him what he wanted.

But oh—she thought it would kill her.

Because she didn't want to face reality. She wanted to hope. She wanted to believe.

She wanted him to love her.

Standing in the shadows of the study, with her arms folded tight around her body as if she could somehow protect her heart, she gave a tearful laugh. *Love* her? Alex thought so little of her that he was willing to break his word for the first time in his adult life, just to get out of their marriage!

If even *he* couldn't keep his marriage vows, then there was nothing left for her to hope for. It was over.

"All right," Rosalie whispered.

At those two words, Alex looked away, his jaw tight.

Tears streamed down her face as she gazed at her husband for the last time. She said thickly, "I would have stayed married to you forever."

"I know," Alex whispered. Taking a deep breath, he cupped her cheek. "That's why I'm letting you go."

CHAPTER TWELVE

The moment the door closed behind Rosalie and his son, the villa went silent. More silent than any house had ever been.

Alex hadn't been able to watch her pack their suitcases. An hour later, his driver took her and the baby away, off to the airport near Venice where his private jet waited.

It was deadly quiet. To celebrate the end of harvest, he'd given his house staff the day off. He went to his study, the last place he'd spoken to Rosalie. He pretended to write emails and read business reports. But he understood nothing he read. His mind was with his wife, replaying the scene over and over, remembering her expression when he'd asked for a divorce.

Now she was gone. Both Rosalie, and his son.

Alex was alone.

He paced the hallways. The villa had never felt so empty before. This place had always been his home. But now, it felt more haunted and desolate than the palazzo in Venice.

Perhaps he should go there, he thought. At least in Venice, he wouldn't hear the echo of his wife's laughter, or his child's babbles. But as he started walking toward the door, he stopped.

No. He had memories of her at the palazzo, as well. It was where they'd first met. Where they'd gotten to know each other. Where he'd first made love to her on their wedding night. No. He couldn't possibly go there, either. His hands clenched at his sides.

Then where?

He should contact his lawyer. Order him to start divorce proceedings. Alex would make sure that Rosalie and his son never wanted for anything, ever. He would give her far more than the prenuptial agreement required. He'd give her half of everything he possessed.

But he knew that was never what she'd wanted from him.

I love you. I would have stayed married to you forever.

Stumbling past the library, he stopped when he saw a dark shadow on the hardwood floor. One of Oliver's toys? Frowning, he went into the room. It was indeed a child's toy, but not his son's. It was a well-loved teddy bear he'd never seen before. Whose could it be?

Then he knew.

"Your wife deserves better than how you're treating her, Alex," Cesare Falconeri had told him last night, when the two men were alone at the bonfire. "You can do better."

It was something that Alex had already known in his heart, something he was trying desperately not to know, so hearing the words spoken aloud had enraged him.

"Your marriage won't last," Alex had responded in a bitter counterattack. "Your children will see your family fall apart. See you break your vows."

"You're wrong." Cesare's eyes had calmly met Alex's. "I'd sooner cut out my own heart than betray those I love."

Now Alex looked at the stuffed teddy bear. He wondered which of Cesare's children it belonged to. Tomorrow, he would ask his assistant to send it on to Lake Como.

But as he was about to set it down, he stopped, looking at the teddy bear, so soft in his hand. For a moment, his heart pounded as he stood in the cool silence of the darkened villa.

His throat hurt.

He would take it himself. Why the hell not? Where else did he have to go?

Anything to get away from the memories of her—

Three hours later, after getting lost twice in the winding roads through the mountains, Alex arrived at the beautiful villa by the lake.

"Alex." Cesare's face was startled when the

butler escorted him into the salon. "What are you doing here?"

Yes, what?

"This," Alex stammered, holding up the teddy bear awkwardly. Cesare took it with a rueful grin.

"You can't imagine how much trouble we had last night, convincing Elena to sleep without it. Thanks."

"Good. Great," Alex said awkwardly. "So. That's it. I'll go."

"Wait." His cousin smiled. "We're about to sit down for dinner. Join us. Come say hello."

And so it was that Alex greeted the Falconeri children, who seemed far more excited by the teddy bear's appearance than his. But Cesare's wife, Emma, hugged him close, before she glanced behind him.

"Where are Rosalie and Oliver?"

"Gone," he said. "Back to California."

His voice was strangled. He'd had to force the words from his throat.

"What? Why?" Emma cried.

Cesare, looking at Alex's face, intervened, "Emma, my dear, would you mind starting dinner without me?" Grabbing a bottle and two highball glasses, he looked back at Alex. "Let's go out on the terrace."

An hour later, deep into his second glass of forty-year-old Scotch, Alex found himself sitting on a terrace overlooking sparkling Lake Como, beneath the setting sun with a slight chill in the air, spilling his guts.

"Don't you see?" Alex finished. "They all died. No matter what I do. Whether I keep my promises or not, I destroy the life of anyone who gets close to me." He'd never thought he'd share the story with Cesare. "I tried to keep my promise to Rosalie," he said in a low voice. "I failed. I can't take care of her like she needs. I can't love her. I don't know how."

"I didn't know how, either," Cesare admitted, looking out at the water. Then, with a smile, he glanced behind him at the joyous villa, full of life. "But then I did."

Alex swallowed against the lump in his throat. "How did you get past it? Everything that happened? The way we were raised?"

Cesare poured his own second glass of Scotch. "You never really get past it." He looked at his cousin, then deliberately held up his glass. "Unless you want to."

"It can't be that simple."

"It isn't." He looked at his raised toast. "And it is."

Tilting back his head, Cesare drank deeply.

Alex looked at his cousin. He suddenly envied the man with all his heart. "It is easy for you to say," he growled. "I saw how you and Emma love each other, but I told myself it wouldn't last. I had to believe that. Because I don't know what love is or what it's supposed to feel like. That's why I couldn't stand to be around you, Cesare. Because it showed me—"

"What you thought you'd never have?" He leaned forward in his chair on the terrace. "I realized I loved Emma when I understood her happiness was more important to me than my pride. More important than anything."

"But I don't love Rosalie. That's the whole problem. I can't."

"You know you're in love not just by the way you feel, but by the way you act. For the first time in my life, I cared about someone else more than myself."

"Then I definitely don't love her," Alex said flatly. "Because all I've done is break her heart."

His cousin tilted his head. "So why did you let her go?"

"Because—because I couldn't stand to see her so unhappy. Because she deserves better than me. Because…"

"Because her happiness is more important to you than your own."

Alex stared at him.

Could it really be that simple?

He'd set her free because he couldn't bear for her to be unhappy. He'd sacrificed not just his honor, not just his comfort, but everything he'd ever wanted—a family, a home, a child, a wife.

He thought again of the loneliness of the villa

after she'd left. His total misery. But he'd been willing to live like that.

For her.

Some people proved their love by proposing marriage, he realized. He'd proved his by asking Rosalie for a divorce.

"Do you see?" Cesare said, leaning forward intently. His eyes crinkled. "Do you finally understand?"

Alex sucked in his breath. "Yes," he whispered.

His actions proved his love.

All the emotion he'd been afraid of feeling, he suddenly felt all at once. It was as if his heart cracked open. He saw the beauty of the Italian lake beyond the villa's terrace, in a whirl of blue and gold and red and green. He saw his older cousin's concern, which Cesare had always had for him, ever since he was a child. Closing his eyes, he saw his own baby's sweet face.

And Rosalie's. Her beautiful eyes, her open heart, her joy in the world.

I love you. He heard the echo of her trembling voice.

She'd known great pain, but she'd still been brave enough to risk her heart, in spite of all Alex's demands to the contrary. In spite of the way he'd neglected and avoided her so he wouldn't have to face his own feelings. She'd loved him through it all.

And now she'd gone back to California alone,

to face her grief over her parents' deaths and the devastation of her childhood home. She was actually thinking of selling land that had been in her family for a hundred years. She'd asked him to go with her, to be her comfort and support. He'd refused like a coward.

So she'd had the courage to do it alone.

Part of Alex had always seen her strength. It was why he'd chased her to Mont-Saint-Michel. Why he'd brought her back to Venice. Why he'd married her, in spite of having believed he'd never marry again. Because some part of him had known, from the very beginning, that Rosalie was braver. That she was stronger and finer than he.

Some part of him had known, even then, that he needed her.

"I love her," Alex breathed, rising unsteadily from his chair.

His cousin, still seated with his hands folded, looked up at him quietly. "Of course you do."

"I have to see her now, today," Alex said. "I have to reach her before she makes a decision she'll regret—"

"Call her."

He shook his head, a lump in his throat. "If she hangs up, it's over. I have to see her in person. I can't let her face everything alone." He remembered how she'd insisted on accompanying him to the charity ball that he'd dreaded. How she'd endured labor, how she'd needed him there, how she'd squeezed his hand so hard. "But how can I show her? How can I prove—" His eyes went wide. "I'll take a plane."

The thought made his heart race, and not in a good way. But even as he started to turn, intending to run toward his Ferrari, he stopped. "It's too late."

"What?"

"My jet is gone. She's taking it back to California right now." Alex set his jaw. "I'll get a commercial flight." Even as he spoke the words, the horizon seemed to swim in front of his eyes. "But that will take too long, maybe even another whole day—"

"Need a plane?" Cesare asked with a lazy grin. "I might have one around."

Alex turned to him eagerly. "Yes. If you don't mind… I've had some…trouble." He licked his lips. "I know it's not rational. But for the last ten years, I haven't been able to get on a plane."

"No wonder, after what happened," his cousin said quietly. He brightened. "Perhaps I can help with that too."

"How?"

Cesare gave a low laugh. "I can punch you in the face till you pass out, then tie you up and toss you on my plane. If you want."

For a moment, Alex actually considered it. Then he shook his head.

"No?" Cesare pretended to sigh.

"I will do it sober," Alex said. "For her. Even if I'm scared out of my mind." He clenched his hands at his sides. "She's proven how brave she can be. So can I. For Rosalie. For our son."

And he thought of them, every moment, as he got on Cesare's plane thirty minutes later. As the jet took off, as he thought of his family members who'd died, his fingernails dug into the leather armrests of his seat.

Alex thought of Rosalie. He thought of how desperately she needed him to be strong. How they needed him to be *there.*

And he did it. Without alcohol, sleeping pills or being punched repeatedly in the face by his cousin. Sweating bullets, he arrived at the San Francisco airport fourteen hours later and stepped out into the California sunshine, knowing he'd just changed his world. He'd proved he could be brave too. He could do anything, if it meant he could win his wife back.

But what if Alex was too late?

Stepping out of the rental car in the midmorning light, Rosalie looked out at the ruins of her family farm in the California countryside.

She'd arrived at the San Francisco airport some hours earlier. Exhausted and filled with despair, she'd gotten a hotel room that overlooked the bay so she could try to rest for a while. From the window, she'd looked down at the path where she'd walked when she was pregnant, talking to her unborn child and wishing desperately that she could keep him.

Now she had everything she'd wanted.

What was wrong with her that it wasn't enough? That she still wanted more—that she so desperately wished her husband could have loved her?

I want a divorce.

Every time Rosalie thought back to that moment, she felt sick with grief. Part of her had hoped he would call her on the plane and tell her he'd made a mistake.

But he'd made his decision. He would not, could not love her.

Perhaps Alex had done the brave thing, letting her go, rather than letting their marriage die a slow, painful death. Because she never could have left him. Even if he didn't love her.

I know. That's why I'm letting you go.

Alex had done what she could not do. He'd been willing to face the truth and end the pain.

Now Rosalie prayed she could do the same.

She'd already stopped by the Wildemer Company's office in downtown Sonoma. The office was going to prepare a contract of sale immediately. But before she could force herself to sign it, she knew she had to be brave enough to go to the farm and say goodbye, one last time.

But as she'd come out of the Wildemer offices, pushing her baby in a stroller, she'd passed by a red-haired man coming toward the door.

"Hello, Rosalie."

Shocked, she gasped, "Cody?"

"I heard you were in town. Is this your baby?" Husky in a flannel shirt and jeans, with a wide, friendly face, Cody Kowalski knelt briefly by the stroller, smiling. "And I heard you were married…"

"What are you doing here?"

He straightened. "The same as you, I guess." He looked up at Wildemer's picturesque nineteenth-century office building. "I'm here to pick up the check." He tilted his head. "We're done. We sold."

"You sold your farm?" she cried. "But why?"

"My parents want to retire to Florida." Cody grinned. "And I hate farming. I always have."

"What?" she exclaimed.

He shook his head. "For my whole life, I tried to be brave enough to tell my parents I didn't want to do it." He looked at her. "All this time I've been wishing I could have been brave enough to do what you did, Rosalie."

"But I never should have left." She looked down at her baby in the stroller, feeling suddenly near tears. "At least you were here, to help your parents escape the fire…"

"No, Rosalie. It wasn't me." He came closer, his freckled face sad. "Your parents did that."

"My parents?"

"They helped us escape. I was in the basement, playing video games. My parents were in the kitchen, arguing. Your parents came and pounded on the door, and told us to leave. If not for them, we wouldn't have known. We wouldn't have made it. They said they were going back to try to save all their animals… They knew about the danger. But they didn't care."

"They knew?" Rosalie whispered.

Cody looked down. "I wanted to tell you at the funeral. But I was scared."

"Why?"

"Because it was my fault," he said in a low voice, wiping his eyes. "My fault your parents died. If I'd just been honest with my parents that I didn't want the farm, they would have sold up long before." He paused. "And your parents would still be alive, because they wouldn't have wasted time coming to warn us."

"It's not your fault."

"But—"

"It was never your fault, Cody. Never. Just be happy. It's what they would have wanted. It's what I want too." She hugged Cody hard as she whispered, "Thank you for telling me."

* * *

Now, remembering, Rosalie looked out at the land.

All this time, she'd thought of her parents' deaths with guilt and shame, blaming herself. Now she was able to see they'd died as they'd lived—on their own terms, making the world a better place.

Just as Rosalie could, if she tried. She took a deep breath.

Everything had burned. Nothing was left, except the house's foundation buried deep in the earth, and even that was covered with ash and scarred by smoke. Looking down at her baby, she said, "This is where I grew up, Oliver. Your grandparents and their grandparents too. I wanted you to see it. Even though it's gone."

Rosalie couldn't run the farm alone. She couldn't. It was the people she'd loved who'd made the land beautiful to her. Without them, there was nothing. She'd lost them forever. Her parents. Her dreams. And Alex—

Looking down, Rosalie saw tiny green shoots, pushing through the rubble and debris.

Or were they really gone?

She'd come to say goodbye.

But she couldn't.

Because she suddenly realized the people she loved were still here, in her heart. In her memory. She could feel her parents' love, all around her.

Love never died. Even her love for Alex, regardless of their divorce, would always be a part of her heart.

Rosalie looked up at the sky. "I will do everything I can," she whispered to her parents. "For you. And Oliver will know how much you would have loved him."

She couldn't sell. She had to stay. It was what her parents would have wanted.

No. It was what *she* wanted.

Turning as she wiped her tears, she saw Alex standing quietly behind her.

Was he a dream? He had to be. Because Alex Falconeri couldn't possibly have come across half the world on a ship in a single day…

"Rosalie," he said huskily, coming forward. He stopped when he was just two feet away from her.

"What? How?"

"I took a plane."

"A plane?" she gasped.

"I couldn't let you go." Taking her into his arms, he looked down at her, his dark eyes intent. "I've been waiting here for you. Because I knew you wouldn't sell. Not without coming to say goodbye."

"How did you know?"

"Because I know you." Alex gave a crooked smile. "I know your heart. And you would want Oliver to see your home. You'd want to know you'd faced it."

"You knew that?" Rosalie hadn't been sure herself that she'd be brave enough.

"You're the strongest person I know." He cradled her cheek. "When you left Italy yesterday, it nearly destroyed me. All I want is to be the man you deserve. The man you fell in love with. So I got on a plane to tell you." He paused, then said in a low voice, "Loving you gave me courage."

"What?" she said through numb lips. "What did you say?"

Alex smiled down at her. "I love you, Rosalie." He ran his hand through her dark hair. "It took losing you for me to realize how stupid I've been. And talking to my cousin..."

"You spoke with Cesare?" she said, astonished. At his nod, she added, "I thought he was your *second* cousin?"

"A cousin is a cousin." He grinned, then sobered as he took her hand in his own. "And family is family. I thought I didn't have the capacity to love because my parents hated each other. But the truth was, I was just afraid to care, after losing everyone I cared about. I was a coward."

"Coward?" She looked up at him in shock. "You got on a plane."

"I couldn't lose you. That's the only thing that made me brave enough. I'd face anything, do anything, to win you back. I want to be your family, Rosalie. Not a stranger." Looking at her, he whispered, "I want to give you everything."

Trembling, she looked up at him.

"But am I too late?" Alex's soul was vulnerable in his dark eyes. "Have I destroyed any chance to win you back, to love you forever? Can you ever forgive what I've done to us?"

With a choked sob, she lifted up on her toes, autumn leaves crunching beneath her boots as she cupped his unshaven cheek.

"There's nothing to forgive. You're mine, as I am yours. My friend. Lover. Partner. Husband." Glancing down at their baby in the stroller, she smiled through her tears. Looking up at Alex, she said, "I love you."

"I'm so in love with you, Rosalie—" With an intake of breath, Alex pulled her to him tightly. And as he lowered his lips to hers, to ravage her in a kiss, Rosalie heard the birdsong and soft sigh of the wind through distant trees, and she knew that, beneath the ash and ruin of her home, new life had just begun. It would grow back, even better and brighter than she'd ever dreamed.

The secret of life, as in making omelets, was love.

Spring had come to Venice at last.

Alex looked out the window of the palazzo. After a cold, dark, wet winter, the city had burst into the flowers of May. In the courtyard below, the leaves were green, and the canal sparkled blue against the sky.

His palazzo, too, had changed.

Looking around the salon where he'd first met Rosalie, when she'd been a panicked, pregnant stranger, Alex smiled. The floor was covered with his son's toys. Oliver was almost nine months old now, and a very fast crawler. He was already learning to walk.

Their family had only arrived a few weeks ago. They'd spent most of the winter planning their new vineyard in Sonoma, where they were rebuilding Rosalie's childhood home, and had passed the early spring at his vineyard in La Tesora. They looked forward to splitting their time between California and northern Italy, and had excellent employees to help manage both.

But Rosalie was his true partner. He'd never felt so alive as he did now. Their marriage had lots of laughter and joy by day—and by night, they set the world on fire. Alex shivered. Saying he loved his wife was insufficient. She was his life.

Everywhere he looked now, he could see her influence. She made everything joyful. The palazzo that had once been so empty and barren had become a comfortable, warm home.

Even Alex's work had changed. She'd convinced him to stop trying to be an anonymous wine genius, losing money every month, and start trying to market Falconeri wines, and turn it into a viable business.

"I know you're a billionaire and don't actually need the money," she'd said, rolling her eyes, "but if we're going to all the trouble of making it, why don't we also try to actually make people want to buy it? Just for fun?"

So they'd returned to Venice to open a tasting room for tourists. Just yesterday, they'd met with an architect to discuss plans for a tasting room and retail store at La Tesora. They might even sponsor next year's Venice Film Festival, to build the Falconeri brand. It made him nervous, but as his wife had said, the paparazzi were following them anyway—why not take that publicity and turn it into something positive? They were making wines. Instead of keeping it a closely held secret, why not go big, and see if the rest of the world liked their wines too?

It was risky. It involved putting his heart, and his wine, on the line. But in spite of that—or maybe because of it—Alex had never been happier.

In the palazzo's salon, above the marble fireplace, the painting of his haughty ancestor had been replaced by a beautiful new oil painting of his wife, holding their baby in her arms. After he'd begged, Rosalie had arranged it as a gift for his thirty-sixth birthday. Alex looked up at the painting, at her dark, spectacular beauty, at the glowing warmth of her deep brown eyes.

Then he heard her voice behind him. "There you are."

Turning, Alex saw his wife, even more beautiful in person. Coming forward, he kissed her. "Is everything ready?"

"Yes. Just in time too." She gave him a sideways glance. "Are you sure you're ready for this? There are four now, you know. *Four.*"

He paused. He'd invited Cesare and Emma and their children to stay not just for dinner, but for an entire weekend. If it went well, Alex and Rosalie and Oliver would go stay for a whole week with them in Lake Como later this summer. "If this works, our children will grow up as best friends."

"But there will be five children in our house at once," she pointed out. "All under the age of nine. Are you ready for that?"

"Absolutely," Alex said.

She hesitated, then watched his face. "And six?" she said slowly. "Could you handle six?"

Alex frowned. "What do you—" Then his expression changed. He breathed, "Are you saying…"

Rosalie nodded shyly. "Around Christmas."

"A baby!" With a shout, he pulled her into his arms, then kissed her cheeks and eyelids and forehead until she pulled away with a laugh.

"You're squashing me!" Her eyes grew wistful. "Are you truly happy, Alex?"

"So happy, *cara*," he whispered, holding her

tenderly. "So very, very happy." He gave a low laugh. "And I'm happy that this time, we did it the old-fashioned way."

"This time," she said huskily, her dark eyes warm. "And all the times to come."

And as Alex lowered his head to kiss her, he was thinking that six children wasn't such a bad idea. Because there was only one thing in the world more important than making wine, more important than promises, more important even than land that had been in the family for a hundred years. Only one thing would last forever, until all the stars went dim in the sky.

Love.

* * * * *

Wrapped up in the drama of
Claiming the Virgin's Baby?
Dive back into Jennie Lucas's passionate world
with these other stories!

The Baby the Billionaire Demands
Chosen as the Sheikh's Royal Bride
Christmas Baby for the Greek
Her Boss's One-Night Baby

Available now!